WOMAN IN THE WIND

THE PREDATOR / PREY THRILLER SERIES
BOOK 4

VALERIE BRANDY

Published by: Emerald Lion Press, 23901 Calabasas Rd., Ste 2088, Calabasas, CA 91302. emeraldlionpress@gmail.com

ISBN: 978-1-964161-18-1

Cover designed by Stuart Bache. Copy Editing provided by Sharon Lennon-Mehlschau and Linda Triol. Photo of the author by David Mueller.

Printed in the United States of America. Visit the author's website and sign up for her mailing list at: www.valeriebrandy.com

❀ Created with Vellum

CONTENTS

AUTHOR'S NOTE

Before Zoe and Mike met, he was in an unwilling relationship— one he didn't consent to— that wouldn't end. A relationship with a woman...

Named *Cassandra*.

This is her story.

1

———

CASSANDRA

I 've been through a thousand ordinary days with Mike. Days where I watched him brush his teeth, unseen beneath the window of his second-story apartment. Days where I crouched behind a shrub outside his building as he leaned against his balcony railing, noting the way he looked out at the city skyline with a question in his eyes. He doesn't ever see me, but I see him, and that's what matters. I've shared the most mundane moments of Mike's life with him, quietly buzzing in the background. I've cherished every ordinary, banal second spent hovering in his orbit, sucking up the nectar of his life like it was something precious, something rare. Some people might call my actions "stalking," but Mike and I have history. He put me through hell. If anyone deserves to follow him without judgment, it's me.

Yes, together, Mike and I have conquered countless ordinary days. *But today is going to be special.*

I'm following his beat-up commercial van as it careens down the 101 South bound when the feeling strikes me. There's a strange crackle in the air. The promise of something to come. The engine in my old Volkswagen makes a terrible clanking sound the whole way there, as if it knows what I'm up to and wants to make its disapproval known. *Don't die on me*, I think. *Not today.* I'm worried about it giving out on me because I have a gut instinct that something special is going to happen today. Some kind of ordinary magic. I can sense it.

Based on his actions, Mike doesn't sense anything out of the ordinary at all. He drives to work the same way he usually does, stops for the same bagel and cream cheese, the same coffee-- black. I watch him through the windows of the shop, my car parked tandem behind another one to so he won't recognize. He doesn't seem to sense anything out of the ordinary— his lack of sensitivity comes as no surprise. He's never had my insight, my whimsy. Mike is a sensory creature, existing only in the tangible world at his "fingertips.

He *does* pause at the register after paying for his coffee, adding an extra tip in the jar. Two dollars more than normal.

Maybe he feels it too, I think, sinking lower in the driver's seat. *Maybe he can sense there's something strange about today.* I like the idea. It makes me feel less alone.

2

"THE ONE"

Cassandra doesn't know she is rarely alone.

And that's because I follow her.

When life doesn't give her a natural reason to be in my field of view, I seek her out.

Right now, I'm watching her crouched in the seat of her car, thinking she's invisible outside the parking lot of a bagel shop. I'm across the street in my beat-up old Chevy, taking a hit on my vape pen with the window down.

She's following that man again, I think.

She follows him often.

He's like a bad hobby. Some people play tennis, or pickle ball, or take up knitting. Cassandra likes to follow this man.

Isn't it funny how a person can be so focused on one thing, that they entirely miss something even more important? Cassandra is so busy following this man, that she's never noticed me.

The problem with Cassandra is she lacks purpose. She follows this man with no real plan. She lets the wind blow her in the direction of the object of her desire, without thought as to what she might accomplish.

But I follow *her* with intention.

The intention to make her mine.

I am her future, and she will soon realize there is only *one* person who is meant for her. *One* other being who understands her darkness. She will forget this man, because I have a plan, and I'm waiting for her.

When I follow her I am nameless. But make no mistake. I am—

"The one."

3

CASSANDRA

Mike unlocks the door to his van outside the coffee shop, revving the engine and peeling away from the curb. As he makes a hard left, the profile of his face comes into view, making me inhale. The moment feels like a slap. Certain angles in his jaw still bring back memories, reminding me of the love we once had.

If we were still talking, I'd ask you, I think. *I'd ask you if you feel the buzz in the air like I do. I know you would say 'no,' but I would ask you anyway, just to feel seen.*

That's exactly what it is, too. A buzz in the air. An electrical pulse. A sign something remarkable is about to happen. Even the weather seems to agree. It's October and overcast here in the San Fernando Valley— no surprise there. But the sky is the strangest shade of yellow. It looks like someone dipped the sky in tea, letting it go all brown and orange and soft. Anyone else would say it's just the smog. The Valley gets cold at night and warm in the morning, making the pollution mix with clean air in the basin between the mountains. Anyone else would blame the weather on environmental factors. But not me. I've always been sensitive to changes in my environment, aware of shifts other people can't see. And it's not because I'm psychic— no. It's just because I'm exactly like a bee.

Not in my form. But in my personality. Bees use antennas to track pollen-- I use my instincts to track Mike. They buzz where you least want them-- I go where I'm unwanted. Their stingers can burn-- my hands can hurt.

Bees and I have everything in common.

I first noticed the similarity between myself and bees sometime after Mike and I broke up. Our relationship was special. We shared a home together, that I decorated in every color. Mike tolerated my ups and downs, but when the downs got to be too much— he left me.

I didn't believe we were really over until the moving van arrived. Mike had threatened to leave me before, but never went through with it. He didn't tell me it was happening— not really. Until the moving van came, all he'd said was "we need to break up." He didn't tell me a date. Or a time.

It wasn't until two burly men entered our apartment and began pushing the hand-carved kitchen table he'd made out the front door that I realized Mike actually meant the thing he'd said about breaking up. I sat cross-legged in the living room as they removed every sign of Mike, leaving only what belonged to me. When it was all done, Mike bent down and said something to me about calling my family. He said he'd reached out to them, and I should as well. He gave me a paper and muttered something about next steps that could "help me." I don't remember what it said, because I threw it in the trash after he left.

I think I sat cross-legged on that kitchen floor for the entire night. Weeks went by, and I *didn't* call my family.

But I landed on my feet eventually. I found a cheaper place in the valley. But I was still heartbroken and searching

— searching for an explanation, trying to make sense of what happened. It was kind of like when soldiers come back from war, and they're not sure where they fit inside their old lives. I'd look around and think, "*This isn't where I belong. I must've stepped into someone else's shoes on accident.*" But then I'd look down and see my own feet.

To make sense of it all, I would wander down the Boulevard during the day, going for walks to ease my mind. I wasn't looking for a book on bugs when one found me. I'd never had an interest in bugs in the slightest. But a few days after Mike and I broke up, I was walking down the street— thinking about him— when a display case outside a library stopped me in my tracks. There was a book on the center shelf, leaning on its side. It was a normal book, except for one thing:

There was a watercolor image of a *bee* on its cover.

She was mid-flight, her winds spread wide, fuzzy stripes a blur as she rushed toward something to buzz around. Her eyes were squinted at an anxious angle. She was focused on nothing but what awaited her in the distance, some unseen object outside the crop of the cover.

I know how she feels, I thought, picturing Mike, and how I couldn't imagine my life without him

"Twenty-five" cents," a sing-song voice emerged from behind a table. I didn't realize I'd even picked up the book, but I must have because it was in my hands. The woman smiled at me, adjusting the plastic name tag on her blouse, her straight, dark hair falling perfectly over her shoulders. The name tag read Kelly Lan, Librarian's Assistant.

I didn't even know librarians *had* assistants.

"Only a quarter?" I asked, gasping as if she was offering me the deal of a century on a book I didn't even want.

"We're clearing space. Everyone has their e-readers

nowadays. Got to keep shelves open for the newest books. The books people really want."

The last sentence shot through me like an electric current. *The books people really want.*

The unwanted books would be discarded. Discarded just like me.

I looked down at the picture of the bee, noticing for the first time how lonely she seemed. She had been abandoned by a previous owner, left to rot in the bargain bin at a library sale.

"I'll take it," I said, digging through my bag for a quarter.

The woman smiled at me. "Enjoy it—" she started to say, but I was already halfway down the block, thinking about insects and quarters, and how we can tell what's meant for us from what isn't.

I spent the rest of the night reading about bees. Their habits. Their likes and dislikes. The miracle of their flight, and how scientists are still not sure how the physics work.

Bees captivated me. Bees made me realize my buzzing wasn't wrong— it was just part of my nature. It was because of bees that I learned to trust my own instincts. Bees have incredible senses. Their antennae tell them everything about the outside world, processing thousands of pieces of information in a matter of seconds.

Now, as I follow Mike's van around a car in the slow lane, I know it's because of bees that I trust my instincts. It's why I *know* today is going to be important. My antennae are quivering, all because of Mike. He is my world — the object I buzz around— and I'm sensitive to every change, every crackle in his orbit. We do everything together. Today, something big is waiting for us. I just don't know what, yet.

His van exits the freeway and grabs the connection to another highway, hopping onto the 405 South. *The ocean,* I think, sensing the salt in the air outside my open window. *So it's the sea, today.*

Mike and I have been on many adventures together, from the rolling hills of Silverlake to the pristine sidewalks of Beverly Hills. Mike travels all over the city, selling his hand-crafted, artisan-made furniture. He doesn't know it, but I like to think of myself as his helpful assistant. I park outside the venues he delivers to— trendy bars, hotels, celebrity talent agencies, spas, and even private mansions— keeping a lookout to make sure the pieces he left in his truck remain safe. Ornate coffee tables. Leather couches with brass hardware punching the cushions in place. Mike can't afford private security, but it would be a worthwhile expense. Each piece he designs is unique-- a one-of-a-kind work of art. Damage, vandalism, or theft could ruin months of work. That's why I always make sure I'm nearby, close enough to keep watch. Sometimes, if I think I can get away with it without being seen, I even walk over to the van and peek inside to get a look at the furniture within.

I wonder if the people Mike sells his art to appreciate it the way I do. If they *love* it like I do. It seems unlikely. His customers are rich. They want his furniture simply because it is the best. The price-tag and the bragging rights are the main appeal. Not the art. Not the craftsmanship. Not a connection with the man who made it.

I love Mike's pieces so much that I keep a rolling list of where he sells his items. The spa off of Beverly. The mansion near 3rd street. The investment group in Holly-wood. Sometimes, I even visit the businesses weeks after a sale to make sure the pieces are being treated well. I step into the lobby and act casual, all while eyeing up the wooden loveseat Mike left there two months ago, or the end table he sold last year. I examine each piece with care, running my fingers over smooth marble tops, peeking under surfaces to make sure no gum has been left behind by bored children waiting for their parents.

Follow-up. It's important, in business. Yes, I am a good assistant to Mike. Not that he ever bothers to notice.

His van makes a hard right, and suddenly we're pulling up to the exterior of an ornate hotel, situated on a prime piece of real estate in Santa Monica that overlooks the beach. The hotel is an older establishment. The kind of place people say has "character." Its windows are framed by delicate wooden shutters, the door a grand, twelve-foot expanse of solid mahogany. The exterior paint is faded in some places— a fragile, juicy shade of merlot that hinted at the opulence of a long-forgotten time. A cranberry-colored rug stretches across the entrance toward the parking lot, which is shaped like a semi-circle to make space for the valet. Nearby, wrought-iron lamp- posts loom over the entrance, their Edison bulbs standing guard like sentinels. I imagine how they might look at night, glittering golden against the darkness, welcoming guests home at all hours of the evening and never asking about their crimes.

It's impossible to deny: this hotel is the perfect venue for Mike's furniture. There's an air about it that embodies his aesthetic— hard and soft, old and new, all at the same time.

I hate it, I think, suddenly jealous of the building. It will receive all Mike's attention for the next hour, and even own a piece of his work. How unfair.

I watch as Mike pulls his van up to the valet, looking horribly out of place among the Teslas and the Mercedes. The valet motions toward the back of the building— the entrance for deliveries.

That's right, Mike, I think, hunkering down behind the steering wheel as his van passes my car. *Can't you see they*

don't appreciate you? Not like I do. They treat you like you're
beneath them.

Mike would never admit to such a thing, of course. To him, all people are the same. His own lack of prejudice made him blind to everyone else's.

I quietly pull my car out of the driveway and circle the block, looking for an inconspicuous parking spot that will allow me to walk back to the hotel. I pass multiple open meters— too exposed— stopping only when I spot an open space between two large trucks. One of the trucks is parked crooked, crossing the white line, making the space almost impossible to use. This is why the spot is empty— it presents a terrible option for anyone who cares about his car.

Thankfully, I don't care about my car. My car is a disaster. A wrecked, twisted, mess of a thing, good only for the sole purpose of following Mike.

I pull into the spot. I try the handle on the driver's side, but the doors won't open. There's not enough space between my car and the truck beside me. No problem. I push on the old moonroof, a sliding window on the ceiling with no automatic function. It opens, letting in outside air. I pull myself up, scooting out the roof and sliding down the back window toward sweet freedom.

"Nice," a man with messy hair grins at me, shifting his skateboard into his other arm. His tank-top hangs too loose around the armpits— an odd, sand-rat style that makes me wonder why he even bothered to wear a shirt at all. His smile, though-- that takes me by surprise. It's angel-white and gleaming, a warm invitation. I don't talk to other people often. I stay away, preferring instead to insulate myself from the pain that inevitably follows attachment. It's nice, to get a smile from a stranger.

"Had to do something," I nod at him, watching as he skates away, wondering where he's going and if someone out there loves him the way I love Mike.

I check my watch. Finding a parking space has stolen ten precious minutes— valuable time with Mike that I'll never get back. My feet burn in my shoes as I run toward the hotel, arriving at its grand entrance out of breath and wheezing. The valet nods at me as if my arrival is the most natural thing in the world— expected even. He holds up a hand and pushes open the tall, wooden doors.

I was worried that I might stick out, here, given the hotel's grandeur, but the beach comes to my rescue. When I enter the lobby, all the guests are in flip-flops and casual wear. The only hint of status comes from the designer sunglasses decorating their faces, labels like *Balenciaga* and *Tiffany* stamped across minimalist frames.

I scan the lobby for Mike, but don't see him. My heart pounds in my chest, like it always does when I can't spot him in a crowd.

What if I've lost him? I think, pained at the idea. It's happened before. Losing track of Mike means there'd be nothing to do but go back to his apartment building and sit outside, waiting for his arrival, sometimes for hours. It wouldn't be the waiting— the boredom— that would make the process unbearable. No, it would be the anxiety of the separation. Mike is a part of my identity, and separating from him is like cutting off a leg.

I take a seat on a plush, blue couch, noticing a stain on the ancient fabric. My legs cross as I pick up a magazine and pretend to read, feigning a confidence I don't feel. While pretending to scan an article on herbal teas, I take in the hotel. It's clear they take good care of it. And yet, there's a distinct feeling the building is rebelling. The baseboards are clean, but the heavy drapes are dusty. There's a kind of mustiness about the place that can only be accumulated over decades of use. It's old. Its exterior is remarkable, but misleading. This is a hotel that used to be magnificent a very long time ago. It's in need of an update, and Mike's furniture will be the first step toward a more contemporary look. *I hope they know how lucky they are, to have him here.*

Across the lobby, a familiar silhouette appears. It's Mike, and even though he's behind the front desk— face darkened in shadow— I can tell it's him. I know his essence, the way his presence holds space in any room. I can identify his outline a mile away.

He steps back, and now I can see that he's smiling. It's his rarest smile— one I haven't spotted in awhile. It's the one he makes when something captivates him. I can tell it apart from his other smiles because it's the only one that makes his eyes crinkle at the corners. I wonder what could have triggered it. A huge sale, maybe? A rare piece of furniture? Mike loves historical pieces. He once went crazy in a thrift store when he found an old chair that had been carved by the Amish a century before.

His shoulder turns, and suddenly I see what he's smiling at. It's not an object. It's not furniture.

It's a woman.

She isn't very tall. Not especially pretty, either— at least not in my opinion. But there's something athletic in the way she moves. She's toned and looks outdoorsy. She has that "comes-from-the-inside" confidence people get when they're in sync with nature and accept the world as it is. The easy, flexible movement of an athlete. She reaches out and touches his hand, but pulls it back just as fast, like she's burned herself. As they walk together, she moves toward and away from Mike like a rubber band, pulling him closer and pushing him away from one moment to the next. There's a stable aloofness about her. She strikes me as the sort of person who would be okay traveling the country while living out of a van. And she might let a boyfriend travel with her, but only if she gets to decide on the route. She's the type who needs someone grounded, someone reliable, to offset her adventurous nature. The kind of person who wants roots and freedom in equal measure.

She would be difficult. Impossible to please, which is always Mike's type. I should know— it's what made him go for me.

No, I think, rising from my spot on the sofa. I want to run between them, to stop this terrible connection from forming. But then I remember that I'm in public. Revealing my presence and violating Mike's restraining order in front of dozens of witnesses would have dire consequences. I stop myself. I pretend to stretch, biting my tongue to keep from calling out. Across the room, Mike holds open a door for the woman, releasing them both into the back parking lot.

The door shuts behind them, and suddenly all sound leaves the room. My heartbeat throbs in my neck, letting me know I'm still breathing, still alive. Still able to feel the weight of a terrible truth.

Mike has just met somebody he might be able to love. Somebody who isn't me.

4

———

"THE ONE"

Cassandra doesn't see me at the hotel's lobby bar. I've ordered a martini, dirty, and the bartender served it up quick. Good man.

I watch as Cassandra clocks the position of the man she follows. He's talking to a woman now, and she looks bothered by it. She's wearing the kind of dazed expression that crosses a person's face after they've been slapped.

She must love this man. Or at least, she thinks she loves this man. Perhaps that's why she follows him. *Love.*

I am different than Cassandra. It isn't love I'm seeking. I'm on a quest for validation.

Cassandra has rejected me once. She fails to see what makes me special. And now, it is my goal to become the focus of her affection. If Cassandra comes to me— willingly — and realizes the value I provide, I've been right all along. I am someone special, and if Cassandra recognizes this fact, I can repair the part of me she broke when she rejected me.

She's standing up now, inching across the hotel lobby toward the front doors. Her pace quickens, like she's trying to catch her breath. I sip my Martini, pleased at this new development.

Cassandra may be upset that the man she follows is flirting with another woman, but it might be the best thing that's happened to either one of us.

5

———

CASSANDRA

I run from the hotel, trying to catch my breath. The valet doesn't wave hello as I streak past. I'm too fast, a motion blur. The sun hits my cheek as I pour onto the concrete, the warm, bright air a stark contrast against the dark interior of the hotel. My feet lead me around back toward the delivery entrance— the place where Mike will be.

I crouch low at the corner of the building, peeking into the parking lot. Luck is on my side. Mike is talking to the woman in front of his van, the doors in the back wide open. Between us, dozens of cars provide camouflage, concealing me from view. I can use them to get closer.

My hands scrape against the rough asphalt as I crawl between the cars, checking windows to make sure they're empty. This is the staff parking lot, and everyone has already started their shifts. There won't be anyone around to point out my presence. I crouch behind a blue Prius, barely within earshot of Mike.

I need to know what you're saying to her, I send my thoughts toward Mike, using the side-mirror of the car beside me to catch a glimpse of their faces.

"It's all from one piece of wood?" the woman asks, impressed.

"It is," Mike confirms, motioning at the back of the van. Inside sits a massive, carved table that could serve as a greeting piece in the reception area. Delicate flowers drip down its side, chiseled in scrolls and loops around the table legs. "They drop it off in one giant block. Takes three guys to lift it. Then the fun part starts."

"And you really do it all by hand?" the woman says, a teasing edge to her voice. "Be careful how you answer. I might have to call the Better Business Bureau if I find out you're engaging in false advertising."

"You caught me," Mike answers, throwing his hands in the air like a criminal. "It's all done by robots."

The woman laughs. She runs her fingers over the curves, each one distinct, carved to perfection. She traces every outline, lips parting as if in whispered conversation with the desk. "No," she says, suddenly serious. "You did this yourself. I can tell."

"How?" Mike says, nervous. "Most people tell me they can't see the difference. Might as well have bought it at Ikea."

"No," she shakes her head. "It's alive."

Great, I think, silently cursing her for saying the perfect thing. Now he'll definitely fall in love with her. Mike can't resist a woman who knows art when she sees it.

"You love your work," she says, her eyes piercing straight through him.

"It's a job," Mike shrugs as if his life's work means nothing. "A strange way to pay the bills. There are days I think I should have done something more practical."

"But you love this," she repeats.

He nods, touched. "I really do."

"I feel the same way about my hotel," the woman turns and motions

lovingly at the building behind her like a mother looking at her child. "It's not mine, technically— "

"But it might as well be," Mike finishes the thought for her.

"Exactly," she nods. There's a silent moment, like she's thinking of adding something. But then, she stops herself. She clears her throat and takes a step back, suddenly uncomfortable. "I'll have Jacob show you where to put it."

"The front desk, no problem," Mike says, a little surprised at the way she switches gears, her voice all business now. "I can haul away the old one if you want."

"Is it much trouble?" She sounds concerned at the idea of putting him out.

"Definitely not," Mike lies. I've seen him refuse to do haul-away about a thousand times. He even puts a note to that affect on his website. He hates how often customers request removal of an old piece, and rants privately about not being a haul-away service. Apparently when the customer is a woman he likes, the rules go out the window.

"Thank you," she smiles. "Maybe I'll see you again. You can come check on your work."

"I never do," Mike answers honestly. "It's too sad, sometimes, to see that it's really been re-homed. They're like pets."

Don't do it, I think, telepathically sending Mike my message. *Don't invite this woman into our lives.*

I can see him gearing up for it— the big ask. A date.

"I'll make sure to take it for a walk when I can," the woman answers, giving him an opening, a final chance to make his move.

"Actually," Mike smiles, his eyes impossibly warm. "If

you're looking to walk a real pet, I volunteer at an animal shelter every weekend. If you join me tomorrow, I'll buy you lunch afterward to thank you for your service."

You idiot! I mentally curse him, shooting invisible daggers through the air.

"Just doing your part for the community?" The woman teases. The smile tugging at the corners of her mouth makes me want to vomit.

"Exactly," Mike nods, playing along. "I care about the world. Always trying to give back. It has nothing to do with spending time with the beautiful hotel manager who likes furniture."

"It's a date," she answers. They start talking about arrangements— exchanging numbers, planning a time— but I don't hear any of it.

I crawl away from the parking lot, my heart pounding in my ears, face red with rage. I've spent so long supporting Mike. Even when he didn't want me, I was there, waiting in the shadows, putting my own life on hold so I could lift him up.

He abandoned me. He ruined my life. And now he has the nerve to start again with someone else? Sure, he's gone on dates here and there since we've separated— but nothing has ever stuck. He's even had a handful of meaningless one-night stands with women he never spoke to again. By all common logic, there's no reason to worry about this new woman. She'll probably come and go like all the others did. But as much as I try to talk myself out of it— as much as I try to explain away my fears— I know, deep down in my bones, that this is real. My antennae tremble, sensing one simple truth:

She's the one for him.

My feet slap against the pavement as I run back to my

car, mind racing, wheels spinning. Acid bubbles up in my stomach, burning my throat. I have to stop this romance from happening. I have to make sure they never get together. I need to crush this relationship before it even begins. A plan develops, easing my anxiety, and promising me a future alone with Mike.

I will find out everything about this woman and use it against her, I think.

I will follow her like I follow Mike, and eventually, some dark, sticky tidbit from her past will arise, giving me ammunition to destroy the budding connection.

My new goal: I will make sure they never end up together. I will end their relationship before it even has a chance to start.

She is my new target, I smile as I reach my car, keys in hand. *A new flower to buzz around.* When I sting her, she won't know what hit her.

I'm about to open the car door when a hand closes around my arm. I whirl around, face-to-face with a large, pot-bellied man, his hair balding in all the wrong places.

"What the fuck," he says, spit flying. "What were you thinking when you parked this way?"

He motions to my Volkswagen, and suddenly I understand. He's the owner of the truck that parked crooked—the one I squeezed in next to. He expects me to be frightened of him. He *wants* a fight Good. So do I.

"I could ask you the same thing," I smile sweetly, pointing to his enormous truck, its tires sitting well over the white line.

"There's a dent on my door that wasn't there before," he snarls, standing up a little taller. "You're gonna pay for it, bitch."

Elation pumps through my bloodstream, because the

universe has offered me the perfect outlet at the perfect time. I need this release, this confrontation. A place to put my rage. I don't care if I cause an altercation, or if this leads to a fight. Let him hit me. Who cares? Nothing can hurt me, now. Because nothing could be more painful than watching Mike fall in love with another woman.

"I don't think that will be necessary," I tell him, gripping my keys a little tighter.

I think about what I could do to him, but instead of executing my worst fantasies, I get in the car and drive away. I have more important things to do now, like stop Mike from making the biggest mistake of his life.

Watch out, Zoe, I think. *I'm coming for you.*

6

"THE ONE"

I watched the man who screamed at Cassandra get into his car, peeling out of the parking lot like he didn't just do something that merited retribution. I considered continuing to tail Cassandra, but the man presented too big a temptation— a place to vent my frustration with righteous indignation. I revved my engine and followed him onto the street, keeping a few cars behind to avoid detection.

Now, he's pulling into a gas station. My opportunity has finally arrived. He's parked his truck at a pump, and there's no other cars around. Just a bored attendant sitting behind plexiglass at the gas station's store.

I put my car in park and turn off the engine, the metal music I'm listening to shutting off so suddenly the silence burns my ears. My legs stretch as I open the door and stride across the cement, walking straight up to the man.

I stop right in front of him.

"Yeah?" he asks, as if he knows me.

"You grabbed her arm," I say, smiling. "That wasn't very nice."

He's about to answer me, but in one, swift movement, I

whip my keys across his face, letting the sharpest edges slice across his cheekbone. He steps back, shocked and amazed, hands flying back to protect himself. When he pulls them away, a red, scorching line is left behind, spanning the distance from his nose to his temple.

His body has knocked the gas pump out of the tank and it's laying on the ground, useless and shut off.

The man trembles, but doesn't move. He doesn't try to retaliate, doesn't raise a hand. He doesn't know what to do with me. People rarely do. And like most bullies, he's a coward. Disappointment bubbles up in my chest. He'd come on so strong. I was certain we were headed for a fight. It was a fight I might have lost, but I'd have enjoyed destroying myself a little, using someone else to do it. I would have taken us both down together, making sure neither one of us walked away whole.

"Is that it?" I ask. He doesn't say anything.

Without another word, I turn on my heel, heading back for my car.

"Disappointing," I shake my head at him, sliding my sunglasses over my eyes. The car sinks as I hop into the drivers side, rolling down the window.

"Next time," I shout, "Park straight. And don't ever call another woman "bitch" again."

The engine purrs as I peel out of the parking lot, catching one last glance at the man in my rearview mirror. He's still standing there, stunned and stupid. The look on his face tells me he's shocked, and I take satisfaction in his disorientation. The feeling is a sick pleasure. A kind of drug I can't wait to taste again. Metal blares from my favorite radio station, and I turn the music up, loving the way it burns in my ears.

I feel powerful. Unstoppable.

I consider the situation with Cassandra, and the man she follows. If the man decides to pursue a relationship with the woman he met at the hotel, Cassandra will try to stop the connection from forming. I know her better than she knows herself. She will do everything in her power to keep them apart.

But what if I were to help bring them together? What if I helped bring them towards each other, driving the man further away from Cassandra?

I smile at the idea, feeling like a kid in front of a set of legos. I will move all three of them around like pieces on a board, putting Cassandra right where I want her.

I'm going to make *sure* that man and that woman find each other, no matter what roadblocks Cassandra attempts to put in their way.

7

———

CASSANDRA

My car bumps over the asphalt as I drive in circles around Santa Monica, listening to air whoosh past the open moon-roof. Seagulls cry overhead, swooping low over trashcans in search of a meal. Teenagers carrying surf-boards gather in packs on every street corner. All around me, everyday life continues.

Nobody knows that my world has shattered. And if they did know know, they wouldn't care.

My car squeals as I pull over at a meter in front of a greasy burger shop — the kind with one counter, and nowhere to sit. I don't put any money in the meter. I'm staying close enough in view that if a parking cop gets inter-ested, I'll have time to jump inside and speed away before he writes a ticket. This has been my motto in life since Mike broke up with me. Get away with what you can. Pay the price of living as infrequently as possible.

I order my burger and peel away from the curb ten bucks poorer. I speed back toward the hotel, a paper bag beside me, the smell of processed meat wafting over the dash. The hotel is right where I left it, but this time, its facade looks different It isn't the hopeful, grand place I'd seen before. Instead, it's a dark, ominous mansion: the spot where Mike met someone new.

I wait for hours outside the hotel, parked in the delivery area out back. Soon, the woman will emerge. I just need to be patient. The minutes crawl past. I eat my burger, chewing on the meat, imagining it filling the empty hole inside my chest. Normally, I'd be nervous to be separated from Mike for so long, fearing he'd pack up and leave town overnight so that I'd never be able to find him again. But now, I'm not afraid. He won't leave. Not before getting to know this new woman. Not with a promising date ahead.

The sun sets. The street-lamps flick on. In a slow trickle, hotel employees emerge through the back exit, heading home after a long day. Restaurant staff. The cleaning service. The concierge. When they pass, I sink down low in the drivers' seat, trying to avoid detection. Each departure makes my position more hazardous. With fewer cars in the lot, my Volkswagen is more likely to be identified as an intruder.

A dozen cars exit the parking lot, but still, no sign of the woman. I wonder if I've missed her. Maybe she left the building early? What if I looked away for a second too long, and she managed to sneak past without my knowledge? I scan the lot, wondering which car could be hers. *Is she more of a Prius owner, or a mini-van kind of girl?* It occurs to me that none of the cars may belong to the woman. Maybe the manager is allowed to use the valet, or the spots in the front specifically reserved for guests. Maybe she doesn't park in the staff lot at all.

Just when I'm getting ready to give up and drive away, a familiar figure emerges from the service doors. It's the woman, a coat wrapped tight around her shoulders. She's waving and smiling at someone behind her. She turns, heading in a straight line— right toward my parking spot.

Please don't notice me, I think, sinking lower into the drivers seat. My breath catches in my throat as her footsteps echo outside the drivers' side door. I peer over the rubber strip at the edge of my window. The woman is opening the door to the car parked right next to mine. I can see the edge of her coat. There's a thread loose, dangling, threatening to unravel the entire jacket. If I could pull it, I would.

I shake my head. My breathing quickens. She's so close that I imagine I can smell her perfume.

What are the odds her car would be the one next to mine? It's another sign, another cosmic signal that we're connected, destined to matter to one another whether we like it or not. Our close proximity is the universe's way of telling me that we're meant to go head-to-head in this game of love, and only one of us will come out on top. I intend to make sure it's me.

I wait until I hear her car engine start, noting the sound of her tires crunching over asphalt. When the coast is clear, I sit up and turn my key over in the Volkswagen's ignition, ready for a chase.

Let's unearth your secrets, I smile, eager to learn more about the woman who has charmed the only man I've ever loved. My investigation will be brief, but thorough. Once I discover her secrets, I'll make sure Mike never looks at her the same way again.

8

"THE ONE"

Hours later, and I've searched the internet for every piece of information I can find on both the man Cassandra follows, and the woman who has earned his attention.

The man is Cassandra's ex-boyfriend— no surprise there. He owns a furniture company and volunteers at an animal shelter. His limited social media presence is likely a result of Cassandra's pursuit of him. She isn't subtle in her efforts, like me.

The woman's name is Zoe. Her biography on the hotel website doesn't offer much in the way of personal information, but her credentials in the hospitality business are impressive.

I pull both their photos off the page, positioning them side-by-side. They look "right" together. This match won't be difficult if I can play to what they both desire.

My chair spins as I wheel myself around, looking at the photos I've displayed on my bedroom wall. They're all of Cassandra, taken from a distance. Cassandra at her apartment, sitting on the windowsill. Cassandra at her job, an apron over her clothes, her posture relaxed as she stands behind the checking out counter, waiting for a customer.

The day I met Cassandra, I knew I was meant to be "the one" for her. It was at the home furnishings store, and I watched her put on that same apron, seeing the way it made her eyes sparkle. I recognized her brokeness immediately. I saw the way she longs for things the world keeps at bay. I knew at once we were meant to be together.

And now, I'm one step closer to proving it.

9

CASSANDRA

he woman's name is Zoe.
I learned it when I followed her to her apartment. She parked on the street, then waved at the postman. He called out to her, "How goes it, Zoe?" And all at once, I learned her name. Just like that. As if it were nothing.

Zoe's apartment building is an architectural wonder. It's on Franklin street in Hollywood— a ripe, mystical area. Only a mile away from the magic castle, there's a heaviness to the neighborhood— a sense of wonder. Trees lean too far over the sidewalks, untrimmed and tangled. Houses with spires and shingles look too regal to be dropped in the middle of the city. The buildings are designed with 1930s, old Hollywood glamour in mind. Zoe's building is no exception.

I followed her to its brick exterior—watched her park on the street and wave at that mailman. She grabbed her mail from him, then entered the lobby, which is framed by two clear, glass doors. Her figure turned into a shadow as she ran up the interior steps. I could just make out her form through the stained glass windows, framed by a matrix of wooden panels. One story. Two story. Three. When she didn't appear on the fourth floor, I scanned the windows on the third, praying her unit would be one that faced East. Then, a gift. A light turned on in a window. I knew: it was hers.

Now, I'm camped outside on a bench across the street, watching that light simmer and dance. The sun has set, and now it's nighttime, making that light look stronger-- brighter. There's a pair of curtains blocking my view, but every now and then a shadow passes across the window, and I know it's her.

Zoe.

Is she making dinner? Does she dance, alone in her apartment? Maybe she's calling a friend, or a parent, telling them all about the amazing man she met today. Or maybe she's the kind of person who sits alone with her joy, allowing it to be a sweet, private secret for as long as she can stand it.

I should leave. I should go home and curl into my bed, a re-run of some trash reality TV show playing on the TV, lulling me into numbness. I should leave her alone. I know I should, but I can't.

Instead, I cross my legs and lean back, making myself comfortable on the bench. I throw my coat over my body. It's one I leave in the backseat of my car even though the weather rarely warrants it. I'd like to say I leave it there because I'm the kind of person who's always prepared, but I'm just too lazy to remove it. I took it with me when I moved to the bench, and now, it's making it possible for me to stay. I could sleep in my car, but I had to park around the block. Moving from this bench means losing sight of Zoe. I'm not ready to separate from her, yet.

Suddenly, the light clicks out.

She's going to sleep.

She'll probably dream of Mike. Of her date tomorrow. She'll imagine being the most important thing in his life-- the person he's willing to do anything for. She'll dream of holidays spent together, and romantic trips abroad. Mike will light her dreams on "re. Little does she know, we're dreaming of the same thing.

I curl into a ball, turning horizontal on the bench, using my arm as a pillow and the coat as a blanket. Tears well in my eyes, threatening to spill over. Why did she have to meet Mike? Why did she have to ruin everything?

I'll unearth your secrets and show him what's wrong with you, I think, breath catching in my throat. *He won't want to be with you anymore when he sees the worst of you.* I don't know what's wrong with her yet, but there has to be some-thing-- something that would be a deal-breaker for Mike. I don't what it is, but I plan to find it. She'll meet the same fate I did— he'll see the worst of her, and drop her like a hot rock.

I pull my knees tighter into my chest, making myself as small as possible. Down the street, a figure appears. It's a man, wearing a thick jacket. He stops to root through a trashcan. He's wobbly, not stable on his feet. His search through the trash proves fruitless-- whatever he's seeking, he doesn't find it.

He ambles down the sidewalk, heading toward the bench. My bench.

He pauses when he sees it's occupied. His eyes scan my form, still curled into a ball. He's deciding whether to make a fuss about it.

"You're here?" He asks me, voice throaty. He just wants to know if I'm staying on the bench. But his words hold more subtext for me. Yes, I think, I'm here. Here, outside a stranger's apartment, at the lowest point I've ever reached. I'm here, choosing to stay outside in the cold, because I can't bear to walk away in case I miss something. I'm here, I'm here, I'm here.

"Yes," I say.

He sighs. "You shouldn't be." He says it with such clarity, such authority, that I wonder if he isn't sent as a warning— a soothsayer foreseeing things to come. Before I can ask him, he ambles down the road, looking for a different place to sleep. He doesn't bother me, and I don't bother him. We share the block for the rest of the night— him, and me, and Zoe— all three of us unaware that we're tangled up in the same narrative, orbiting around each other, sending ripples into one another's universe. I've destabilized his world. Zoe has destabilized mine. And now— because it's a law of the universe that everything must come full circle— I'm about to *shatter* hers.

When I wake up, it's to the sound of bus tires screech-ing. A bus pulls up to the bench, its doors opening like a mouth. The stop is a formality: it's too early for weekend travel. The streets are empty. No one gets in or out. The driver makes eye contact with me, surprised to see a new figure on the bench. But he moves on, no questions asked.

I wait for a few hours, eyes fixated on Zoe's window. Eventually, a light flicks on, its glimmer less noticeable in the dawn.

Leave, I think. Leave so I can find my way inside. Leave so I can learn your secrets.

No matter. The delay gives me time to execute my plan. I stand, stretching so my arms reach toward the sky. I lumber toward the trashcan, rooting through for something useful. It's mostly discarded food containers, but I find one item that will do— a plastic straw, red lipstick lining one end. I pull it out and bend it in half.

Casually, I head for the entrance to Zoe's apartment. I need to confirm a suspicion. A simple pull on the double doors proves my gut instinct to be true: it's locked. Most apartment buildings in Los Angeles are. Breaking into a house would be easier. I'll have to be patient.

The wait feels like days, and I spend the time counting pigeons from the steps, watching them root through an abandoned bag of chips. Finally, a small figure appears inside the building's lobby. It's an old woman. She's hunched over, silver hair down to her shoulders. She's quite beautiful in her own way— one of those people that's lit from within. She smiles at me as she opens the doors, almost like she enjoys giving me the benefit of the doubt. It's as if she takes pleasure in trusting another person. In helping them.

"Strange, isn't it?" She says as she opens the doors, motioning for me to take over and grab the handle for myself.

"What?" I ask, voice sharp, half-expecting her to reveal my weaknesses.

"The smog," she glances upward, eyes tilting toward the sky. She's right. That odd, orange glow is back, a dirty, grey reminder that the city is a cesspool, even up high.

"Worst I've seen it," she says, before bouncing down the steps.

That's it. I'm in. I wait until the woman is out of sight, then fold the straw into the smallest shape possible. I shove it in the hole on the side of the door where the lock usually sits. When I let go, it expands to fill the space. I shut the door behind me, wait a second, then pull it open. It's unlocked, now. No one will notice the change. And even if they do, nobody will fix it. This building is full to the brim with tenants, all of them stacked on top of one another. Too many people coming and going creates a dilution of responsibility.

Now, I'll have access to the building whenever I want.

I head for the stairwell, counting the floors as I go. One, two, three. For some reason, I'm worried about running into Zoe, even though she has no idea what I look like. If we met, I could act casual. Pretend I haven't been following her. I could even smile at her, just like that old lady smiled at me. I could comment on the smog. I could pretend to be ordinary.

But I am not ordinary. I know myself. If Zoe crosses my path, I'll do something spontaneous. Something self-sabotaging. Something that ruins the plan I've set in motion, putting emotion before strategy.

Better to avoid running into her at all.

When I reach Zoe's floor, I peak out into the hallway. I make sure it's empty before pushing the stairwell door open, then creep into the hall, careful to keep my footsteps quiet. The floors are lined with a stained, paisley carpet— the kind that used to be thick and lush, but has been flattened over the years. Now, it's balding and faded.

Counting the doors from right to left allows me to zero in on Zoe's place. I have to guess based on the number of windows, but it's easy to estimate that she's somewhere in the middle of the hall. Maybe apartment 167, or 168.

I stand between the two, wondering if she can feel me on the other side. I press my ear against the door to apartment 168, imagining her moving around within.

Silently, like a shadow, I move across the hall and round the corner. I imagine myself as a ghost, sitting on the other side of the wall, waiting, out of sight. It won't be long until she emerges. I know Mike's schedule, and he always volunteers at the dog shelter early in the morning. He starts with his coffee, then a run, then-- the dogs. Zoe will have to leave soon to meet him in time. It won't be long.

Sure enough, a few moments later and I hear the turn of a knob. The door slams behind her. I peak around the corner just in time to see her disappearing down the stairwell. She's smiling to herself, her hair shiny, face glowing. She's wearing makeup today. She wants to impress him.

Try-hard, I think, biting my lip to keep from shouting at her.

When she's out of sight, I head to the apartment she exited. It *was* hers after all. I wonder how I knew. Maybe there's a connection between us I can't see but can feel—some invisible thread running between Zoe and me, its spirals spelling out "Mike, Mike, Mike."

I bend down to examine the door. I know how to pick a lock. It's a habit I picked up after Mike broke up with me and I found myself in the unique position of needing to access his house without his knowledge. Hours of watching Youtube videos taught me that locks are not as unbreakable as most people think. Hearts, though—those are fragile.

The deadbolt is a standard, golden orb. Nothing I can't crack. But the handle is unique. It's made entirely from glass. It might be original to the building. Its odd, hexagonal shape reflects the light, echoing the stained glass windows throughout. There's a tiny hole above it, it for an old-fashioned key. I've never faced a lock like it. I'll have to hope she only bothered to lock the deadbolt.

A piece of my hair tugs at my scalp as I dig into my messy-bun, pulling out a single bobby pin. I unfold it. The deadbolt squeaks when the bobby pin enters its mouth, like it knows I'm an intruder. The secret to picking locks is to and the places where the grooves of the key push the pins into place. When I think I've applied pressure in the right direction, I turn the bobby pin, giving just the right amount of torque. There's a satisfying clicking noise, and I know I've done it. The lock is open.

Now, for the handle. It presents a bigger challenge. I start by checking to see if it's locked. My hand wraps around the crystal orb, turning in both directions. There's a sickening pop, and suddenly the doorknob comes right off the door, settling into my hand.

Her door knob is broken, I think to myself. *I wonder why she doesn't fix it?*

There's a line of some gooey black substance tracing the metal part where the knob meets the door. It's evidence of a pathetic, do-it-yourself fix. The glue tells me everything I need to know about Zoe. Instead of calling the building manager or hiring a handyman to fix her doorknob, she's the kind of woman does it herself with cheap, tacky wood-glue.

I take one last glance around the hallway to make sure no one is watching, then shove the knob back onto the door. As I enter her apartment, the door shuts softly behind me. My chest rises, savoring the scent of someone else's space.

I've done it. *I'm in.*

10

"THE ONE"

Technology is amazing, isn't it?

From the glow of my computer screen, an entire world is available to me.

And that world is one that spins around Cassandra. I login to my GPS tracker app, which I've connected to a source beacon clipped to the bumper of her car. Following her in person is superior and preferable, but a person can only be in so many places at once. I have family commitments. A business to run. The tracker I clipped to Cassandra's bumper allows me to see what she's up to, even when I can't be there in the flash.

A map of the city appears, a flickering blue dot indicating Cassandra's location in the mess of tangled lines that constitutes Los Angeles. There she is. My girl.

The street name looks familiar, and I realize I've seen it just a couple hours earlier while researching Zoe.

Cassandra is at Zoe's apartment, I smile to myself. Cassandra lacks my knack for subtlety. She puts herself in situations that could lead to an arrest or worse. She operates on emotion rather than logic. That's something I'll be able to help her with, when we're finally together.

I take a sip of my soda and watch the blue dot flashing, rhythmic and full of promise. What a fun game we're playing, together. I can't wait to make my next move.

11

CASSANDRA

Zoe's apartment is messier than I expected. I always assume disorganization is my own, unique crime. A fault possessed by no one else. When comparing myself to others, I almost always assume they're cleaner than I am. That's why when I pictured Zoe's place, I imagined a pristine, HGTV ready home. Modern in style. Bare floors. Baskets everywhere to stop potential clutter in its tracks. Like an Ikea showroom floor. *Modern, but sparse, and completely unoriginal.* That's what I pegged her as.

But now, I'm standing in a messy, one-bedroom apartment. Piles of clothes litter the floor, spilling out from an undersized closet. She isn't dirty, but she's definitely not organized. Her only saving grace is the decor style. She's into Bohemian chic. Fabric wall tapestries take up one side of the room, and a brightly-colored poof with tassels on its edge sits by the couch. There's drapes everywhere, giving the vague impression of a circus leaving town. The piles of clothes on the floor only add to the effect, blending into the scene like they were intentionally placed.

I wander through her space, trying to inhabit it as if it

were my own. I'm a bee in another Queen's hive, buzzing around, mapping the landscape. A sticking sound as I open up the refrigerator. It's almost empty, except for a few cans of Coke and some yogurts. Beyond the kitchen island, a small desk takes up a corner of the living room. I run my fingers over the island, making my way toward the desk. A puffy office chair stands behind it. I cross my legs and sit in it, tapping a key on her open laptop. A message pops up on the screen, prompting me to enter a password. I can't access the files inside. That's unfortunate. Most people forget to clear their internet search history, where the most delicious vices hide. Still, I spin around in the office chair, imagining what it feels like to be Zoe.

If I were her, would I live her life better than she does?

The spinning makes my stomach turn. My heels dig into the carpet, slowing my turns.

I stand, still woozy, and head for the bedroom, sprawling out across her Queen-sized bed. My legs warm immediately when I crawl underneath the comforter. It must be all goose feathers inside. It's striped blue and yellow, and looks like something she might order for the hotel. Maybe it is. Maybe she ordered one hundred comforters for their rooms, plus one extra, just for herself. I smush my face into the pillow and inhale. It smells like Pine Trees and Lemon Grass. Her shampoo must be one of those earthy botanical types. Makes sense. She's blessed with the kind of hair that's so thick it can handle abrasive products without breaking. Lucky. If I used a shampoo like that, all my hair would fall out, and I'd end up bald. Might be worth it, to smell the way she does.

My knees pull up to my chest as I lay on my side, taking in my surroundings from the safety of Zoe's bed. Across the room, some picture frames sit on a dresser next to the

TV. There's a photo of Zoe and two girlfriends at the beach, wide sun-hats shielding their faces. They're all smiling like it's the best day they've ever had. Beside it sits a circular frame, featuring a picture of Zoe with a woman older than her. The woman has her nose, and the same pointed chin.

Her Mom.

The picture tugs at some chord inside of me, making me sit up, breathless. It's something about the look in her Mom's eyes. In the photo, she's glancing at Zoe like this girl is the most precious thing in her world. Seeing a picture of Zoe with family humanizes her. It reminds me that she's not just an adversary. She's not just a monster trying to steal Mike from my life. She's a person.

She's somebody's child.

My pulse races, and it takes everything I have not to run from the room. Images of my own parents flash before me, and I wonder what they're doing right now. Are they sitting on the porch, drinking the tea my Mom makes this time of year? What do they tell other people about me? How long will it be before they give up on me once and for all? They would be disappointed in me if they knew my present location. I know that much. It's why I can't answer their calls. Why I *haven't* answered their calls in a very long time. I have nothing good to tell them. But for some reason, they keep trying anyway.

I look back at the picture of Zoe and her Mom, wondering how often they see each other, and if they're close.

You're not hurting Zoe, I remind myself. *Not really. She doesn't even know Mike. She doesn't love him. Not like you do.*

I press my face back into the pillow, inhaling the scent again. I wish I could trade places with Zoe. Maybe if I were more like her, Mike and I would still be together. But I can't change. My only option is to eliminate the competition.

She has to go.

The covers twirl into a tangled mess as I extricate myself from the bed. I rearrange them, trying to make them look the way they did before I arrived. They were a bit of a mess to begin with, and it's hard to copy the haphazard arrangement. I'm forced to settle for an untucked left side, and a smoothed, flat right side. Close enough. She's too messy to notice any minor differences.

Find her secrets, I whisper to myself as I return to searching the apartment.

The carpet cradles my feet as I head back toward the kitchen like an unwilling chef. The drawers are filled with junk— screwdrivers and old photos, parking stickers and pens devoid of ink. There's a couple of sad pans in the cabinets, but mostly, it's empty space. She doesn't cook much.

When the kitchen has been thoroughly vetted, I move onto the living room, checking the cabinets in the TV stand. I don't know exactly what I'm looking for, except that it has to be evidence of one of Mike's deal-breakers.

One benefit of having known Mike for so long is that I know what he finds intolerable. The things he can't live with in a partner. The things that would make him break up with someone. The list is short, because it doesn't take a lot to make Mike happy. He's able to forgive most flaws, except for a few on his deal-breakers list. For example, he can't be with a woman who doesn't like animals. His retirement plan is to get a bunch of dogs and buy some cheap land out in the dessert, creating a dog ranch. He could never date a woman who hates pets.

Maybe she's allergic to dogs, I wonder, knowing it's

unlikely, considering she already agreed to volunteer with him at an animal shelter.

I finish with the TV stand, moving to the desk, running through the deal-breakers list in my mind. Mike can't be with a woman who has no ambition. I know that for sure, because I watched him go out on a couple dates with a pretty hostess who told him she didn't know what she wanted to do with her life. They were halfway through dinner when she said it, their wine glasses still healthy and full. She took a sip, and the merlot stained her lips. "I could see myself traveling, maybe?" The hostess sighed, wistful. "Or like, get a job in each place I stop? Just something temporary, to fill the time."

"But what would that do?" Mike asked her, suddenly disinterested in his chicken picatta. "Would you write a book about it? Or make a blog?"

"I don't know," she shrugged, oblivious to his growing doubts about her. "I don't really know what I want to do, except like, experience the world and have fun."

She smiled at him. He smiled back, but he didn't mean it. I watched his eyes glaze over the moment she let her lack of direction slip, and could practically see the interest fading from his expression. I knew right then: they'd never make it. Of course, that didn't stop him from going up to her apartment afterward. But he left in the morning, and I never saw them together again.

I used to have ambition too, Mike, I think. I used to have plans for my life, until you came along and ruined it.

The trickiest thing about Mike's search for love is that he seeks a contradiction in his girlfriends. He likes instability in a woman— just enough aloofness to keep him guessing. He loves the creative, free-wheeling, adventurous type. But only when it's paired with a motivation to build something meaningful. He's attracted to ambition, and whimsy. But not *too* much whimsy. Too much unpredictability in a mate is a dealbreaker for him. I found that out first-hand when he broke up with me for once trying to run our car on the road in a moment of rage. I wasn't trying to kill us— not really. I just wanted to pull over and grabbed the wheel too hard. The moment brought our relationship full circle. Mike was attracted to me because I was creative and unpredictable, but had ambitions to become an interior designer. I was attending a top design school. I had plans to start my own business. But I also let my emotions rule me. Ambition, and spontaneity. The perfect combination in Mike's eyes. But it was my free-wheeling side that— the same one he loved in the beginning— that ultimately made him leave.

One mistake, forever held against me, I think, rummaging through a desk drawer. I stare at the computer, wishing I could guess Zoe's password and gain access to her emails. I debate the merits of attempting to guess, but it might lock up her computer, making it obvious someone was inside her apartment. Better not to risk it.

After thoroughly searching the desk, I move onto the bookshelf, glancing through the various titles. Most of her books are on the hospitality industry, but there's also some that exist only for recreational reading. There's a series of adventure books, all of which take place in the great outdoors. There's also a couple mysteries. I don't find any classics, or romance books. We have different tastes, apparently. She doesn't read like I do.

There's a pile of mail on one of the lower shelves. It's mostly junk. Some advertisements. A couple of bills. I'm about to pass by it and continue my search, but then something else catches my eye. It's a flower. A single rose. It's turning brown at the edges, curling in on itself like it's ready to die. But she hasn't thrown it out yet. Beneath it sits a card.

I carefully lift the flower off of the card, making sure no petals fall. The card is simple in design, a solid black line on its exterior, printed over linen paper. It's the sort of vague stationary people buy in bulk and use for any occasion. My fingers tremble as I open it, sensing I might have found my smoking gun.

The handwriting is difficult to make out, slanted and angular. Still, I read the words to myself.

"No matter how many times I fail, just know: you are my heart. Don't give up on me. Not yet."

Beneath the card is a simple signature. It's a single letter. "W."

My breath catches in my throat as I search the bookshelf for an envelope with a return address. I don't find one. I empty out the trashcans in case she threw the envelope away, but there's not anything that fis the size of the card. The little mail she's tossed out is generic advertising mate-rial and bank statements. Nothing personal. Nothing hand-addressed. The absence of an envelope makes me think the card wasn't mailed. *It was given in person.*

The rose. The card. The message, "you are my heart." All of it points to one thing:

Zoe is already seeing someone.

I smile as I think about the final dealbreaker on Mike's list, the thing he absolutely can't stand no matter what.

Infidelity.

Granted, Mike and Zoe aren't exclusive yet. It's not a crime for her to accept his invitation for a date when she's got loose ends somewhere else. They've only just met. They're not in a relationship. But this rose could *look* bad if presented at the right moment. It gives me the chance to create a story. A narrative. If Zoe and Mike get closer, and I reveal she's seeing someone else at the proper moment, he'll lose interest in her forever. I'll have to wait until the right time, of course. The best opportunity is when they've grown close, but not too close. I'll wait for the moment Mike lets his guard down. When he first opens up to her in a way that's not casual, but intimate. I'll wait until he's vulnerable, and then I'll pounce. The stakes are high. I'll have to time it right. Too soon and he'll excuse it away as something was happening before they met. Too late and she might end the affair, taking away my only ammunition. The timing must be perfect. I have to pull the trigger before trust has developed between them. That way, their connection won't survive the blow. If I can play it right, it's a good plan. One that will give me back my alone time with Mike. But to carry it out, I'll need evidence. Something Mike can't deny, even if it comes from me. A pivotal question remains.

Who is W.?

12

"THE ONE"

The date between Mike and Zoe is today. And it will go well. It has to. I made sure it would.

All it took was a basic bribe and some excellent research. Through a paid information site, I was able to figure out Mike's home address. From there, I was able to locate three animal shelters in the surrounding area. I called each of them, asking if Mike volunteered there, claiming I wanted to surprise him for his birthday. When I was able to get a confirmation at one of the shelters, I went down in person and introduced myself to an acne-ridden teenager working the front desk.

"You know Mike?" I grinned at him. The kid nodded, trusting me immediately. I dress like a teenager, which makes his generation assume I'm "cool."

"You his friend?" The kid asked without suspicion. No one is ever suspicious of me. It's one of my many gifts. My exterior doesn't match my interior.

"Yup," I said. "He's bringing a date here tomorrow and I need you to make sure it goes well."

"How am I supposed to do that?"

There was a thunking sound as I dropped a tote bag onto the table. The kid opened it, revealing a bottle of champagne, an official-looking certificate, and a circular pin with the words "number one volunteer" etched on the surface.

"Let's make him volunteer of the month," I smiled.

"Uh..." The kid shook his head, annoyed. "We don't really do that here. People just show up and walk the dogs. There's not like, an award or anything.

I expected this. Without a word, I reached into my wallet and pulled out a hundred-dollar bill, sliding it across the desk.

"Make a big fuss, and I'll come back with another hundred. I'm talking applause and shit. Make the man look like a saint. Got it?"

The kid looked at the bill, considering. Then, he grabbed it, shoving it in his pocket. "I've got student loans," he said in explanation.

"Don't we all," I smiled at him. "Thanks again." My feet carried me from the shelter, triumphant, knowing that the date would be a win not just Mike, or the dogs, but for me.

13

CASSANDRA

It's late afternoon when I leave my parking spot outside Zoe's apartment. My Volkswagen sputters down Franklin Boulevard, her building getting smaller and smaller in the rearview mirror. Every cell in my body wants to head toward the animal shelter where Mike volunteers. They'll probably still be there, walking the last of the dogs. I'd love to catch the end of their date— to judge how it went — but I have a thing called a job I have to be at. Saturday through Thursday, I work the register at a cheap home decor store. I don't resent the work. It's as close I'll ever get to becoming a full-fledged designer. But I hate that it interferes with tracking Mike.

You'll be late, I think to myself, searching for a way to justify the detour. *But you'll know what happened. Maybe if you see them together, you'll spend less time following Mike because you'll have some information.*

This is a game I play with myself. I debate the depths of my obsession, promising that a small taste of Mike's world will satiate me instead of making me want more. I'm like the dieter who takes a bite of someone else's dessert to stave of the cravings, but then goes home and eats a whole pie. I could call myself on my bullshit, but I don't. It tastes too good to be bad.

My tires screech as I take a hard right, heading toward the street that points toward the animal shelter.

I'll just make it quick, I think, making myself yet another promise I can't keep.

When I pull up to the shelter, I have to duck down in my seat to avoid being seen. Mike and Zoe are out front, in plain view, just twenty feet away from the parking lot. I circle the block, approaching from the other side, where a large cluster of trees obscures the view. The car groans as I put the car in neutral, coasting forward until I'm situated in a parallel parking spot behind a van. Mike and Zoe are still in front of the building, laughing. If I roll down my window, I might be able to hear them. I sink low in the driver's seat, listening as the glass slips down.

Zoe's voice rings out first.

"You're amazing!" Zoe laughed. "I didn't know I'd be standing here with an *award-winning volunteer.*"

"That was weird," Mike answered. "I promise you I had no idea that was happening..."

"Sure," Zoe teased, her tone skeptical. "You just *happen* to bring me here the day they're honoring you for all your 'incredible work with animals.'"

"I seriously didn't know!"

"They *applauded* you," Zoe continued. "The certificate, the champagne, the badge..." She moved closer to examine something on his shirt. I peaked over the windowsill, watching as she reached for a kind of pin stuck to his t-shirt. *She's too close to him*, I thought, swallowing hard.

"You did look surprised," Zoe said.

"You have to believe me," Mike shook his head. "I didn't

even think they gave out volunteer awards. I've never seen them do that. And even if they do give out awards, I'm not a great volunteer. I'm here like, once a month and that's it. This was..." Mike paused, thinking. "This was really strange." He let the words hang, as if suddenly bothered by something.

"Well, I think you just don't give yourself enough credit," Zoe said. "You must be a great volunteer, because the dogs love you. You're good with them. Especially the little ones. You like them better?"

"How could you tell?" Mike asks, genuinely surprised.

"You zeroed in on all the small ones. The mangier the better. Missing an eye, a tail? Mike's your guy!"

He laughs. "It's true," I hear him say. "I like the little ones better."

Don't tell her why, I think, groaning because I know Mike's about to reveal something personal. He only reveals his weaknesses to people he likes.

"Why?" She asks.

"It's..." he pauses, making me hope he won't open up. But of course, he does. "My family's kind of fucked up."

"That makes you like small dogs better than big ones? If that's true, you'd think there wouldn't be a single small dog left for adoption."

"No," he continues, trying to find the words. "When I was a kid, I had to go live with my aunt and uncle. My aunt didn't really want me there. I just felt like I didn't belong."

"Ah," Zoe says, understanding.

"I guess that's why I like the little ones," Mike adds. "I know what it feels like to be the underdog."

"If it makes you feel better, my family's messed up too," Zoe answers. "How?" Mike asks.

"That's probably a second-date story," Zoe tells him.

She's avoiding the question. It doesn't surprise me. She's more aloof than him, harder to reach. It won't be a turn-off, though. If anything, it'll make him want her more. Mike will eat that shit up.

"Does that mean I *get* a second date?"

There's a long silence.

Maybe she said no.

Carefully, I peak my head over the edge of the window-sill, expecting to see Zoe in mid-thought, or looking away from him, deciding how best to let him down easy. moment. She wraps her arms around him, and he puts a hand on her hips, pulling her closer. Then, they're pressing against the exterior wall of the building like they've been looking for each other their entire lives, two halves of a whole, finally reunited. They're magnets pulled together across a universe, unable to wait another second before meeting once more.

They separate, and Mike says to her, under his breath. "Can I take you somewhere else?"

Zoe looks at him sideways.

"Not like that," Mike covers. "I want to show you my workshop. Where I make the furniture."

"Let's go," Zoe agrees.

He's taking her to his workshop?! I think, rage coursing through my veins. Mike is more protective of his workshop than any place in the world. In his eyes, the workshop is a spiritual center, his place of refuge and peace in an other-wise unreliable world. In the course of our entire relation-ship, I can count on one hand the number of times Mike let me visit him at his workshop. And now he's taking this woman there on their first *date.*

I duck back below the windowsill, heart-racing. Acid bubbles up in my stomach. I start thinking about what my life would be without Mike— what I'll do if he somehow manages to disappear from my view. This girl— she's going to take him away from me. I can feel it. It takes everything I have not to leap out of the car, to run toward Mike and yell at him for ruining everything.

Instead, I turn toward the passenger seat, a sick, sour taste bubbling up in my mouth. I don't even realize I'm throwing up until the vomit hits the floor. When it's done, I'm left alone in a stinking, rotting car that smells like my own bile, tears streaming down my cheeks. I peek over the edge of the windowsill, hoping to catch one last sight of Mike. But they're already gone.

14

———

"THE ONE"

I'm waiting for Cassandra at the home decor store where she works, but she hasn't shown. Rows of glass jars line the walls. Trinkets sit on shelves, waiting to be sold. There's a wooden, familiar smell in the space that never gets old. I like to look at her here, but she never sees me, even though I am in plain view. I don't hide myself, and yet I'm invisible to her.

I know why she's late today. Mike and Zoe had their date at the animal shelter. My mouth arches up into a smile as I imagine how it went. I'm confident it went well, only because I made *sure* it would.

The fact that she's late tells me she's upset. *Good,* I think. Maybe she'll learn to look a little more closely at the people who actually pay attention to her.

I look to my left and right, noticing how busy the store has become. It's always like this on weekends. Single mothers route through kitchen appliances. Bachelor men stand in front of throw pillows, looking put-out. Small children escape the grasp of their parents' wanting hands, running up and down the aisles, creating havoc. I imagine myself as just another face in the crowd, invisible, but powerful, a leopard waiting to pounce. Maybe I'll have a special moment with Cassandra, today. Perhaps she's in the right mindset. What if today is the day— everything changes?

15

CASSANDRA

When I get to work the store is packed with customers, and the manager, Patricia, is already waiting for me. Patricia is twenty-three, has a piercing in her nose, and wants everyone to know she's in a band. She was nice to me when she first hired me, but the feeling has soured. Ever since I declined her invitation to join her at a Ska concert after work, she's decided I'm not deserving enough to be in her good graces.

"You're late," she says, holding out an apron. Everyone here is required to wear aprons, even though we don't bake anything.

"I know," I tell her, lifting the apron over my head.

"My Dad's gonna give the store to my brother if you fuck this up for me," she says, running a hand through her electric-blue hair. "And if you think I'm bad, spend a few shifts working with Tommy."

"He sucks," I agree, even though I've never met her brother. But I have to assume he sucks, because he's related to her.

She snorts at my answer like her she doesn't believe I

mean it, but she leaves me alone, which is all I want anyway.

"Guy on aisle four wants help with the rugs," she calls over her shoulder as she walks away. "He specifically said he wanted an expert with a good eye for design. Guess that's not me." I mentally curse the man. All our rugs are clipped to a circular display on the ceiling. Getting them down requires a ladder, and it's impossible not to get a finger bitten by the snaps.

When I get to the display aisle, the man is already trying to pull one of the rugs down on his own.

"Let me help you with that," I tell him, trying to keep the edge out of my voice. It's annoying when customers take it upon themselves to do my job.

The man whips around, and I get a good look at him for the first time. He's in his mid-forties, not much to look at. He isn't especially strong. Not broad. There's nothing special in his features. He's got a bump on his nose and a very ordinary, square jawline that travels up toward his dark hair. Still, there's something pleasing about his smile. He's well-dressed, like he might have a Pinterest account or read fashion blogs. Cool sneakers adorn his feet. Relaxed jeans and a backwards baseball-cap give an effortless vibe. An indentation on the side of his right cheek gives the effect of a dimple, even though it's likely just an old scar. He smiles at me like he knows me.

"Tried to beat you to it," he says, his voice teasing.

I pull out the store's stepladder and trudge up its metal frame. "This one?" I ask, holding the edge of a hideous beige carpet. As the man nods, I unclip the rug and remind myself that this job is just a way to pay for food and housing.

It gives you flexible hours to follow Mike. That's all.

The man holds onto the edge of the rug while I descend, trying to help me keep my balance.

"Thanks," he says, laying it out across the floor. The beige ugliness stares up at us.

"What do you think?" he asks me.

"I'm supposed to approve of everything in this store, so I love it," I tell him. He laughs as if I'm joking.

"No, really. What do you think? I'm bad with design. I need someone who knows what they're doing." He looks me up and down like he's taking me in. "I have a feeling that's you."

"Where are you going to put it?" I sigh, running through the usual checklist for selling a rug. "Living room?"

"It's for my store, actually," he motions across the strip mall our shop is located in. Through the cloudy windows, I can just make out the exterior of a home security store. I pass it every day, but never bother to look twice. There's an ugly sign outside the front door that reads "WE'RE WATCHING YOU." The exterior hasn't been washed in ages, and the paint has faded from pale green to a hideous grey. The entrance isn't welcoming. The affect is intimidating, to say the least.

"It's bad, I know," the man says, watching my scowl. "The inside is worse."

"Well, a home security store doesn't have to be pretty to be effective," I try. He doesn't buy it.

"Actually, most of our customers are women. Not sure they care if it's pretty, but I've had a couple walk in and turn right around before looking at anything," He scratches his head, like it's a mystery he can't solve. "The interior doesn't have good flow. Guess the gun racks get in the way."

"Sounds... inviting," I laugh, pointing at the cameras stationed outside the entrance. "The cameras help, too.

Everyone wants to feel like they're being watched while they shop."

"It's bad," he agrees. "I've always been great with technology. Not so great with people. Was hoping a rug might warm it up. I think the look of it all is hurting our sales. Women purchase security equipment because they want to feel safe, but if the shop itself is intimidating, they're not coming in."

"Sounds like you need more than a rug," I tell him, wondering what the inside looks like and if it's as bad as I suspect.

"Yeah. When I opened it, all I wanted to do was help people protect their homes. Monitor the place, keeps tabs on their kids. I thought the concept of safety alone would sell it. May have overlooked the importance of presentation. And now that we've done a tally and realized most of our shoppers are women..."

"You keep saying that," I snap at him, suddenly annoyed.

"What?" He steps a back, a little uneasy. "Sorry if I--"

"No, it's "ne," I pause to make sure I say the next part the right way. "It's just-- can I be honest?"

"I need you to be," he says, not in the least bit offended.

"You say the word 'women' like it's an alien species. Like men are the default and women are an anomaly. We're half the population, and we live in a world that's not built for us. The standard size of everything— doors, chairs, windows— it's all built with a man in mind, even though women are generally smaller. The women that come into your store... there's a reason they want to monitor their homes. Some of them feel unsafe. Some of them have been through something terrible. So if they walk in, and the design flow shouts 'this place is not for you,' they're gonna turn right around and go to the nearest Best Buy. Which isn't built for them either, but is at least neutral enough it's more appealing."

"That was—" he's smiling as he answers. It surprises me. "That was really helpful. You're right. I thought a rug would help because I was trying to make it pretty. But it's not just about being pretty. It needs to be functional. It needs to appeal to our customer base but not pander."

"Right," I say. "It's not just about painting things *pink*. It's about figuring out what the main concerns are for the demographic you're catering to, and then putting those items front and center, displayed in such a way it's appealing to them."

He sighs, running a hand through his hair. "Wish I knew a designer who could do it for me. You don't have any you recommend, do you?"

Suddenly, an idea hits me. The space between us narrows, and lightning crackles in the air. My antennae stand upright, sensing something important, something magical.

This man was brought to me for a reason.

"You said you can rig a place with cameras?" I ask him.

"Sure," his eyebrows crunch together like two caterpillars walking inward. "Easy set up if you know what you're doing."

"And you *do* know what you're doing, don't you?" I ask him.

"I'd like to think so," he answers, not sure where I'm going with this.

"I'll make you a deal," I tell him, growing more confident in my plan with each passing second. "I need you to show me how to install security cameras in an apartment. For protection, of course," I add quickly.

"Got a bad ex, huh?" He asks, filling in the blanks.

"You could say that," I confirm without elaborating. "We'll trade. You help me with a security system, and I'll rearrange your store for you. I'll make it appealing."

"You do that kind of thing?" He asks, skeptical.

"I have a degree in interior design. In fact, I arranged everything here," I motion around the immaculate store. It's true. Patricia paid me extra to come in on a weekend. It was a rare project I was passionate about, and it shows. The aisles are arranged for perfect customer access. The decor items are laid out in tiers, by color and function. Sporadic sitting areas provide miniature examples of what could be done— a fake living room, a fake bedroom, all decorated by me and me alone.

The man looks around the store, taking it all in. "Impressive," he says, holding out a hand. "You've got a deal." We shake on it.

"I'm Jerry," he adds.

"Cassandra."

I give the man my phone number, and just when I'm done entering it into his cell, Patricia calls me from the register. There's a long line of customers weaving toward the back of the store. Too long. Patricia can't handle it herself.

Jerry waves goodbye and I take my spot beside Patricia, clicking a second register on to help her fight he deluge of transactions.

"You and me," Patricia glances at me in a rare moment of warmth. "We're set for battle. Ready?"

"Ready," I nod. Then, I motion for the next customer, offering my best winning smile. As I ring up the transaction, and the one after that, and the one after that... I think about what I've achieved, today.

I've found a way to follow Zoe, even when I can't be

there in the flesh. There's a sticky feeling in my chest. It whispers that I'm a hypocrite. That— for all my rants about the world not being made for women— I'm part of a bigger problem. What I'm doing to Zoe— what I feel *entitled* to do — is wrong. And I know it. But I'm sick, and I'm tired, and I didn't design the world we live in. I'm just another person, trying to get what's hers. And I've just found a way to make sure my wrongs are righted.

She'll never escape me now.

16

———

"THE ONE"

We connected, today. Cassandra spoke to so many customers. She endured a world of interaction— a huge accomplishment for an introverted soul. But in the midst of it all, we connected. It was special. I know she felt it too.

My plan is working. She's letting go of Mike. And moving closer... to the one. The one is meant for her.

Me.

17

CASSANDRA

When my shift is over, I stop by Mike's place on my way home. By the time I pull up to his apartment complex, it's dark outside, and the street lamps are flickering on, their dusty bulbs casting an orange glow over cracked sidewalks.

His building is a gated, generic box with square shrubs lining the exterior. It's the kind of place a person rents because it's cheap. I know every nook, every cranny, every secret hiding spot it offers. I've spent so many hours waiting outside the building, exploring its many entrances and exits, that I feel like I live here, too.

I put the car in park and remove my apron, leaving it on the passenger side. I'd be embarrassed if Mike found out where I work. He'd say it's a waste of my potential.

What do you know, about potential? I used to say to him. My changing ambitions frustrated him. One day I'd want to run my own business. The next, I'd dream of moving to New York and working for a posh interior design company that specialized in the latest celebrity trends. I had passion, but not direction. Mike was all about direction. Choosing a path and sticking to it. It was a problem between us. I liked to live for pleasure. I designed for the love of it. I would have designed every day if I could, even if no one paid me a dime. Mike, on the other hand, wanted to make a living from his passion. He saw the world as a thing to be conquered, and I saw it as an experience to be lived.

The neighborhood is quiet, like it usually is this time of night. I don't even bother to cover my face as I cross the street. There's no one around to see me. Nobody to ask questions. I turn the corner and head for the alley that backs up to his complex, stepping on a large dumpster. Above me, a fire escape looms, the edge of a rusty ladder just out of reach. I jump, like I always do, catching its bottom rung in my hand. It rattles as it drops toward me, inviting me upwards as if it approves of my endeavors. Chipped paint breaks off as I climb, leaving little specks on the palms of my hands. When I reach the top, I'm out of breath, but flushed with excitement. I check my watch. It's 7:45pm. Mike will be having a smoke on his balcony. He's a creature of habit, and that nighttime cigarette is an important part of his routine.

The building is shaped like a letter "L," its flat roof creating a ninety-degree angle, making space for a courtyard and swimming pool below. Gravel crunches under my shoes as I move toward the roof's edge. When I reach it, I lay flat on my stomach, peering out over the cement border toward the other side of the building. There, across the courtyard, just a couple of stories down, stands Mike, having a cigarette on his balcony. The smoke moves upward in spirals, and I imagine Mike's thoughts contained within, his answers to me written in some code I can't decipher.

It's pedestrian, the way he smokes. I'm a little disgusted by it.

He leans against the rail. Rubs a temple with one hand. Hikes up his pant leg with the other. I've always hated that habit.

If I'm being honest, there's a lot of things I hate about Mike. The way he looks down on anyone who doesn't have the next thirty years of their life planned out. The way he smokes. The way he's so desperate for others to love him. I try not to dwell on these things, but they're qualities that I've always disliked in him. When he reminds me of their existence, it shakes my insides like an earthquake. It makes me wonder— do I really still love Mike? Or do I just miss him because I got used to him?

How was your day? I ask him, pretending he can hear me, willing him to look my way.

He doesn't. Instead, he just stands there, his expression satisfied, his posture lighter somehow. There's no denying it. He looks different tonight.

It's because of her, isn't it. You're happier now?

He puts out his cigarette sooner than usual. It's still got half a life left in its length, but he pushes it into the ashtray anyway— wasteful, almost like he doesn't need it anymore. He retreats into his apartment, the balcony doors sliding shut behind him. Curtains pull shut across the glass, blocking my view, refusing to allow me to see what's within.

The hive, I think, imagining the interior of Mike's apartment. It's a place that should belong to me, too. A place we should share.

I scoot sideways on the roof, rolling over onto my back, letting the gravel press against my skull. I'm sprawled out in a yoga pose, the one they call *sevasana*— "the corpse pose," — where you don't move at all. My eyes turn upward, taking in the solid night sky. It's an inky tarp smothering the earth, poisoned by city lights, stars made dim by too many artificial bulbs. I focus on the few starts left, tiny pinpricks looking down on me. I trace patterns between them, imagining each as a hole in a honeycomb, a place where I could rest.

We were supposed to build a hive together, I whisper to Mike. *What went wrong?*

He can't hear me, and even if he could, he wouldn't answer. But it still feels good to ask.

18

"THE ONE"

I'm back in my safe space. The hub that is my bedroom. I like to think of it as my lair. In the corner sits my bed, covered in clothes. On the far wall across from the bed, a mini-fridge, stocked with beers, my favorite sodas, and a multitude of snacks— all that I don't have to make the dreaded journey downstairs and interact with other humans. On my desk is my computer— the lens through which I experience what's most important to me. I've always looked at my computer as a portal to any location. Any time. It's a device that allows me to execute my biggest plans and endeavor on my greatest works. I've always loved technology.

I rub my hands together, pulling up a website creation tool. It's easy enough to create a basic site using the drag and drop editor— no need to resort to Java script or code from scratch, although I could, if I wanted to. It takes about half an hour to create the false site, but when I'm done, it looks professionally made. It advertises "LOS ANGELES CHAMBER OF COMMERCE— LOCAL BUSINESS

EVENTS." Underneath, it presents a calendar of events. Most of them are real and verifiable. But one is simply something I've invented. "Date Night in the City, Sponsored by Local Business Owners." Beneath is a list of real businesses, all of them false sponsors.

I move on to the fake email account I've created, opening a draft for a new email and typing an address into the "to" field. It's an address my research tells me belongs to Mike.

This is Mike's lucky week, I think. Not only has he been given an award by the animal shelter, he's about to win some free shit, compliments of the Los Angeles Chamber of Commerce.

I craft the email carefully, re-reading my work when I'm happy with what I've done.

"Congratulations! The Los Angeles Chamber of Commerce has selected you as the monthly winner of our Date Night in the City event! Take a trip around Los Angeles' favorite hot spots in one night, compliments of the Chamber of Commerce. Your date is on us."

Beneath the paragraph, I've listed a complete date night with stops within blocks of each other, along with a digital gift card to each location. *Enzo's,* an Italian Restaurant in Silverlake is up first, followed by *Purple Rose,* an ice-cream shop just down the block. There's a gift card to the movie theater further down the street, and the entire evening has been comped by yours truly.

Mike will never know, of course. He'll just think he's won— a randomly selected entrant. And on a carpenter's salary, he'll need the help. It doesn't hurt that I've chosen locations consistent with what I've been able to discover about Zoe's favorite items. She loves Italian food, as evidence by her Instagram feed, and brags about the Purple Rose ice-cream shop on her Facebook page.

It's almost too good to be true— because it is.

19

CASSANDRA

It's early when I meet Jerry outside his security store. Only a few cars are arranged in the strip mall's parking lot. Most of them are outside the donut shop, a bell clanging every time someone opens its dirty front door.

"The coffee's not bad, but the donuts are always stale," Jerry says, keys rattling in his hand. He's been unlocking the shop's front door for what feels like an eternity. First the security screen, then the deadbolt, then the handle, then the *other* deadbolt.

"Do you really need this many locks?"

He shakes his head like he feels sorry for me. "You've had a great life if you can walk around trusting people in this world. Me? I know what people are capable of. Better to prevent a thousand crimes that weren't going to happen than be unprepared for the one that does."

The corner of his eye twitches as he says it, and for the first time, I realize that what I thought was a dimple on his cheek is actually the end of a long line. It trails from his cheek to his temple. It's a faint pink, more noticeable when the sun shines on his skin.

"You've seen some things then, huh?" I ask him.

"Yes," he says, and we leave at that.

The door pops open, and Jerry leads me into a window-less, damp, jail-cell of a shop. Gun racks block the middle of the aisles. Wire mesh keeps customers separated from wall displays of pepper spray. At the back of the store, a collection of security cameras are pointed at the entrance, all of them broadcasting what they see onto little TVs. A thousand versions of myself stare back at me, making me feel like I'm drunk and looking in a mirror.

"Wow, Jerry," I sigh. "You didn't tell me it would be *so* charming."

"It's bad," he agrees. "But we've got a lot to offer. Top of the line technology. No place safer. Just gotta make it look that way." He pauses, chewing on the inside of his cheek. "What's your advice?" He motions around the space like we're guests on a home design show.

"Not so fast. First, the goods."

He smiles, then leads me toward the back wall. The images on the TV change as we mov closer to the cameras, my face doubling in size.

"I recommend something that connects to your phone." He picks a camera no bigger than a baby bird off the display wall and passes it to me. "You can check it when you're not there, and the battery life is pretty solid."

"I need something smaller. Something she can't see."

Jerry's eyebrows raise. "You didn't tell the pet-sitter she'd be on camera?" There's a long, uncomfortable silence. I've told Jerry I need cameras in my apartment to check in on my pets during a vacation, because the truth would scare him away. For a second, I think about being honest with him.

I'm planning to video my ex's new love interest without her knowledge so I can keep tabs on her whereabouts and discover her darkest secrets, I imagine saying.

Instead, I stick with the lie. "Do I *have* to tell her?"

"Legally, yes. You always have to tell someone they're being recorded. Ethically... I don't know," Jerry shrugs. "Makes you wonder if they might change their behavior, doesn't it? Can't tell you how many parents come in to buy nanny cams. The stuff they catch when the babysitters think they're not watching would make you sick."

"Do you have kids?" I ask him. He takes a step back at the question, and suddenly I realize I've made the situation too personal. I do that, sometimes.

"Yes," he admits at me. "And when my son was little, I hid a nanny-cam in my house and didn't tell a soul it was there. But that's just me."

"So you think it's okay, then?"

"I can't say either way. But if you think she could be hurting the pets..."

"My dog was weird when I got home from the last trip," I assure him, trying to look pained about the emotional state of an animal that doesn't exist.

"Well, then, there's only one way to find out, isn't there?" He pauses, contemplating. Then, he motions toward a second door in the corner— one I'd assumed led to a storage closet. "I only show this stuff to the good guys," he says, unlocking the handle. "Seems to me you're one of them."

He doesn't say it as a question, but I feel the need to answer anyway. All I can muster is a nod. It's enough.

The door swings open, revealing a tiny room with shelving on the walls. Lights flash. LED screens blink. In the corner, a mannequin wears a full kevlar suit, complete with a face shield.

"If you take anything from this room, you didn't get from me," he says, pointing to a shelf on the side wall. "Over there's your best bet."

I run my hands over the edge of the shelf. It's filled with ordinary objects. A pen. A lamp. A sculpture. A lapel pin. A notebook.

"These aren't..."

Before I can finish the sentence, Jerry pulls out his cellphone and shows me the screen. My own face stares back at me.

"This feed is coming from the pen," he says, picking it up and passing it to me.

"What about audio?" I ask, wondering how something so small can provide any results at all.

He turns up the volume on his phone. My own voice rings back at me, contorted but recognizable. "*What about the audio, audio, audio*?" My words echo in a never-ending feedback loop.

He mutes the phone again. "Five second delay," he says. "You'll capture everything happening in real-time. You can even set it to notify you when there's motion detected. And the pen is so tiny, no one will notice it. You can put it on a desk, leave it there, and see everything that happens. Plus," he smiles, taking the pen back from me and pressing a button on its end. "It actually writes." He scribbles on his hand and a line of ink appears.

"This stuff would really help me," I say, sure I can't afford it.

"Just get this place looking better and you can have whatever you want."

"Your sales are hurting, huh?" I ask.

He doesn't answer, but the look in his eyes says it all.

"How long do you think you need to pull this place together?" he asks, a concerned furrow in his brows.

"Two days," I shrug, imagining what the space could be, when I'm finished. "I'll just need to buzz around a bit." He nods, and together, we get to work.

IT DOESN'T TAKE us long to tear the place apart. Guns leave their shelves. The TVs are unplugged. We clean the store from top to bottom, piling everything on one side of the space, leaving the interior naked and ready for change. Throughout it all, Jerry looks pained, watching his life's work deconstructed into its most essential parts. But for me — this is heaven. Nectar pumps through my bloodstream, making my cheeks flush, making my heart pound.

This is what I was made to do, I think to myself as I push a display case across the room, imbibed with a sudden, super-human strength. *I was made to turn pollen into honey. To make hives and honeycombs.*

When we've officially taken everything apart, it's time to put it together again in a new way.

"Customers are coming to your store because they want to feel safe," I tell him, imagining myself as one of his clients. "They don't want to walk in and be intimidated. We need to put the comforting things in the front, and the tough stuff in the back."

Together, we arrive at an arrangement that makes sense. Jerry chooses items he would recommend to a novice in self-defense— pepper sprays and security signs— to move to the front of the store. Other items, like guns and electric fencing, go in the back.

When the basic arrangement is done, we create a plan to warm the space up with furniture. A rug here. A couch there. The discussions are specific. We talk colors and details, so Jerry knows what to buy. We agree on a color scheme of blue and grey. "It's calming," I tell him. "It will help customers feel relaxed." We agree on creating a sitting area specifically for consultations, so he can wrangle customers the second they walk in the door. We get so deep into specifics that it feels like we own the store together. It becomes a shared passion, a mutual project— something we both love and adore.

Later in the day, we visit the home decor shop I work at to look for wall art. We sort through the clearance aisle together, debating the merits of each piece, each style. I suggest something impressionist, soft and fuzzy. Jerry likes contemporary, strong and bold. We compromise on a set of abstract prints that echo our selected color scheme.

It feels like we're moving into together, I think. I can't help but smile at the idea. I'm struck by the fact that I haven't thought of Mike all day. Not once.

When we get back to the shop, Jerry's hangs the art pieces up with a hammer and some determination. It takes awhile to get them straight, but when the job is done, they warm the space up. "You were right," he says, relieved and surprised. "It just needed some color."

"You should play music, too," I tell him. "Something instrumental. Something relaxing."

We stop for dinner. Jerry orders a pizza, and we eat it cross-legged on the floor. There's still piles of items to get through, but the store is coming together.

"Why did you open this place?" I ask him, mouth full.

"Wanted to make people a bit safer, I guess." He pauses like he's wondering if he should tell me something. "Actually, I was the victim of a crime once."

"No you weren't," I say, shaking my head. "You're too— aware."

"I was," he turns his head to the side, pointing out the line on his cheek I noticed earlier. "I was a teenager when it happened. I was sitting in my family's front yard. I'd gotten in a fight with my parents, just needed some air. I was sitting there, and this man walks up to me."

"Did he try to rob you?" I ask.

Jerry shakes his head. "No. He just came up and asked me where the bus stop was. He seemed a little— *off*— but I thought maybe he was just lost. I was in the middle of giving him directions when he pulled out a razor- blade."

"No," I gasp.

"Yes," Jerry says. "He sliced my cheek. Then he walked away." Jerry goes quiet for a minute. "Funny thing was, the whole thing happened because I was mad at my parents. And now, I don't even remember what we were fighting about. They called an ambulance. All of us forget how pissed off we were in the bustle of it all."

"Why did the man cut you?"

"Who knows," Jerry shrugs. "Maybe he was on drugs. Maybe he was sick. You can't think too much about the 'why' with something like that. You gotta just trust the universe has some divine order to it."

If there were order in the universe, Mike and I would still be together, I want to say. I bite back the words, focusing on Jerry instead.

"Do you hate him?" I'm not sure why the answer is important to me, but for some reason, I'm filled with an urgent need to know what Jerry thinks of the man who hurt him.

"Sometimes I did, especially when I was in college. Took twelve plastic surgeries to make me this beautiful," he points at the scar, still there, still deep. "Shocking, I know. So yeah, I hated him for awhile for putting me through all this pain. But now? Now I just feel sorry for him."

"Sorry for him?"

"Sure. A person has to be really twisted to do a thing like that. His head is not a place I'd wanna be." Jerry finishes his pizza, wiping his hands on his jeans. "That's why I opened this place. Decided I wanted to keep people safe from all the weirdos out there."

My throat tightens. The thought is impossible to push away.

I'm one of those weirdos, I think.

"Speaking of, time to trade," he smiles at me, then disappears into the back. He returns with the pen. "You earned it."

"We're not done yet," I say, suddenly desperate to spend more time with Jerry. "The front entrance still needs work."

"The door?" His eyes crinkle as he looks at the security screen. We've left it open to let in some fresh air.

"Sure," I say, grasping. "Curb appeal. Doesn't matter how great we make the inside if nobody likes it from the street."

"Hmm, good point," he scratches his chin, tone serious. "I propose another trade. You help me with the exterior, and I'll come to your place and set this thing up for you. Show you how to connect it to your phone, where to put it for the best reception— the whole nine yards. VIP service. What do you think?"

"Perfect," I say. My voice is calm, but something ugly churns inside me. To help me set up the pen, Jerry will have to go to an apartment that's not mine. Zoe's apartment. The one I've broken into. The one I've invaded. I'm no better than the man who cut his cheek. I'm the criminal, the monster, the exact kind of person he's trying to protect against. Worse, I'm involving him in my crime. The thought comes again, no matter how hard I try to push it away.

I'm everything he hates.

Without thinking, I reach up and trace the line on Jerry's face, letting my fingertips follow it from start to end. Looking at it makes me want to cry.

"I'm really sorry that happened to you," I say.

The closeness is strange. It's a new barrier broken between us. Some soft, sweet introduction to an intimacy that could grow. His eyebrows raise at the intrusion, his cheek burning against the cool graze of my hand— but he doesn't move away.

"I'm not," he says, not bothering to explain further. I remove my hand from his face, embarrassed at how forward I've been. If he feels the same, he doesn't show it.

"Now it's time for me to keep up my end of the bargain," he says. He leans in a little, and suddenly I think he might kiss me, but I move my face away before he can reach me.

"I'm patient," I say, stuttering. "You can help me with the tech side of things any time."

"I'm patient, too," he smiles, and I feel like he isn't talking about our deal anymore.

20

"THE ONE"

S he hasn't come to me yet. But I can wait. I am patient. When Cassandra feels Mike slipping away from her, she will move in my direction. If I move too quickly— if I push her— I'll lose the small progress I've made so far. The best things in life take time.

21

CASSANDRA

I'm on a date, but it isn't mine.

My fingers clutch the wrapper of my greasy fast-food taco, and I try to make myself even smaller in the back-seat of my car. I'm parked at a metered spot on the edge of the curb, on a city block in the trendiest part of Silverlake. Outside my window sits a perfect view of an Italian restaurant called *Enzo's*. Through the glass front doors, candles flicker and white tablecloths adorn the space. This restaurant is hardly Mike's taste. It must have been a place Zoe wanted to go.

They're visible through the side window, but only barely. Mike's back is turned to me, and Zoe's face comes in and out view as leans to her left and right, occasionally blocked my Mike's stupid, fat head.

Move over so I can see her! I think, trying to send Mike a telepathic message. He doesn't move. He's always been a dense.

I take another bite of my taco, thinking about how Mike has changed. We used to eat greasy fast food together, and he never took me to a fancy restaurant— in part because we never had the money. Now that his business is doing better, I guess he's traded up. Maybe I was his "starter girlfriend," and Zoe is the real prize.

Zoe moves into view, and I'm surprised to see she isn't smiling. In fact, she's spitting something out into her white cloth napkin, looking a little horrified. A waiter comes over. He's talking to them, his expression angry. Mike points at Zoe's plate and she holds it up as if she's trying to explain something. The waiter shakes his head and throws his hands in the air as if to say "what am I supposed to do about it?"

There's something wrong with their food, I realized. The sound of my own laughter surprises me. I lay flat on the back seat of my car, clutching my stomach as I laugh. Leave it to Mike to pick an expensive restaurant that serves absolute garbage. The man doesn't have an upscale bone in his body. With Mike's taste, Zoe will be lucky if she doesn't get food poisoning later.

I sit up, peaking over the edge of the backseat window. The waiter has brought the check in a black plastic folio. Mike opens it up. He says something to the waiter. He's holding a printed piece of paper that has a barcode on it.

No, I think, shaking my head. *Mike... you are not trying to use a coupon right now.* Mike slides the piece of paper into the folio, handing it back to the waiter, who looks confused but doesn't question further.

Maybe it's not a coupon. This establishment doesn't seem like the type of place to accept such a thing. I wonder if Mike bought a gift certificate online before coming the restaurant? What a weird way to pay. It's classic Mike, though, to make such a blunder. He's all practical and no beauty. He doesn't understand the romance in a man pulling out his wallet and paying for a date— in his utilitarian eye, a gift card and his credit card are the same thing.

For a moment, I feel sorry for Zoe. This date can't be going the way she'd hoped. As a woman, I know the pain of a failed romantic endeavor. But the feeling of pity fades when they exit the restaurant moments later, and I see her reach for his hand— a gesture that reminds me she is, in fact, my enemy.

They're heading toward me. Straight toward me.

I sink down lower in the backseat, but bravely risk rolling down the window so I might hear what they say as they pass by.

"Call me crazy that I don't want hair with my fettuc-cine..." Zoe says, the hint of a laugh in her voice.

"I'm so sorry," Mike interjects. There's genuine regret in his words. "I'd never been here before and when I won the date night I just thought..."

"Don't be silly!" Zoe exclaims. "It's not your fault. It's just part of the adventure. Now we have a great second date story about how we got in a fight with the waiter at one of LA's worst Italian restaurants."

"My other gift card is for ice-cream," Mike says, his voice fading from earshot. "Should we see if we can burn the place down?"

I don't hear Zoe's response because now they're too far away from me. They've moved out of earshot down the side-walk, heading for a crosswalk. The light turns green and I watch as they cross the street, making a right turn and disappearing from view.

It's now or never.

I leap from the car and slam the door shut behind me. My legs carry me forward and I put the hood on my sweat-shirt up over my head, placing my hands in my pockets.

There's other pedestrians out tonight, and I try to blend in with the flow off foot-traffic, crossing the street just as Mike and Zoe did.

It takes me a beat to spot them and for a moment I'm afraid I lost them. But then I notice Mike, his tall frame standing in line outside an ice cream shop. It's a trendy establishment— the kind of place that serves unusual flavors like eggplant and lavender. A neon sign in a violet shade flickers above an ivy-colored wall, spelling out the store's name: "PURPLE ROSE."

The line weaves all the way down the street for two city blocks, snaking its way across the sidewalk. Outside, hipsters wearing fedoras and high-waisted shorts take pictures of themselves in front of the shop, presumably to post on social media. Mike and Zoe are at the end of the line.

I can get closer, I think, moving toward them. No one seems to notice as I slip into the line, a mere two people away from Mike and Zoe. The couple in front of me doesn't think anything of it as I lean in to hear what Mike's saying.

"Really long... looks like an hour. But I'm happy to wait in line if you are."

"No, no, we can stay!" Zoe says. "I don't want to ruin the big night you planned."

"I didn't plan it," Mike says. "The Chamber of Commerce did." He pauses, and I can see a realization in his eyes, like something important has just hit him. "You know what?" he says. "Fuck the Chamber of Commerce. I'm taking you to *my* favorite place."

He grabs Zoe's hand and pulls her from the line. She follows him, surprised but willing. There's a pain in my chest as I realize what's happening.

Mike is letting Zoe get to know the *real* him. The one

who hates trendy spots like *PURPLE ROSE* and snooty restaurants like *Enzo's.* That means he's serious about her.

My eyes burn as I exit the line and speed-walk back to my car, determined to follow them to wherever they're going next. I won't be left behind. Mike *can't* leave me behind.

Not again.

A SHORT CAR RIDE LATER, and I'm strolling through a terrible part of town. The kind of place where you keep your keys in your hand as a makeshift weapon when walking late at night. I've left my car parked down the block, and am heading towards the place I know Mike has taken Zoe. I realized where he was headed as soon as we exited the freeway— it's a familiar stop, and I've followed Mike here many times before. He comes here when he's lonely or upset. It's open 24/7. Mike gets upset a lot, so it's a kind of emotional support crutch on his worst days.

I can't believe he brought her here, I think, angry at Mike that he never thought to invite me to his secret spot. It's a place he only started frequenting after we broke up, but still — he could have asked *me.*

I make a left and spot the place I'm seeking: a churro shop, its simple storefront a metal bar, the scent of burned sugar clinging to the air. There's a couple of sad tables outside. At one of them sit Mike and Zoe, each of them holding a churro in hand.

I pull my sweatshirt tighter over my head and dip into the open-air clothing store next door. Cheap dresses hang on the wall, bordered by nylon shirts. Nothing costs more than ten dollars. A sales girl chewing gum tries to approach me, but I wave her away. I move toward the clearance racks that overflow onto the sidewalk, pretending to look through one so I can listen to what Mike and Zoe are saying.

"You're right," Zoe laughs. "This is way better than ice cream."

"I come here a lot," Mike says. "It makes me feel alright about everything."

"How often do you feel like things aren't alright?" Zoe asks. I roll my eyes. Who does she think she is— his therapist?

"A lot of the time," Mike shrugs. Leave it to him to be honest. Doesn't he know you're supposed to pretend to be a well-adjusted adult during the first few dates. "But right now, I have to be honest— feels like things are looking up." He smiles at her.

There's a pause as Zoe takes the opportunity to say something I can tell she's been waiting to say. It's there in her eyes, like a question. "I hope it's okay— I get to know people slowly," Zoe says. "I've just been through a lot and I really like you, but I don't want you to think it's weird if I'm not fast to open up. It's not because of you, it's just..."

"The world?" Mike asks, nodding as if he understands. "Hey, that's okay," he puts his hands up. "I can take my time. Carpenters don't have a reputation for being impatient."

"Is that so?"

"Kind of the opposite, actually," he says. "We take our time. Roll through life. Let me be your friend first and see where it takes us."

"Where do you think it's taking us?" Zoe smiles.

"To the point where you find me completely, utterly irresistible," Mike says as if it's obvious. "It's just what happens, I can't even help it--"

He's about to say more, but Zoe leans in and cuts him off

with a kiss. She presses against him and the world disappears, like it's just the two of them and nobody else exists.

Including me.

When they part, she stays close to him, whispering
under her breath. "I think we can be more than friends."

They kiss again and slip away from the store, walking
back to my car with my head down. Tears burn my cheeks,
because it's undeniable that my initial suspicion was
correct, and this connection is real. It's a moving train that
has to be stopped, and I need ammunition to do it. For a
moment, I wonder if it's wrong to attempt to destroy a
connection that could make Mike's life better. He's lonely.
That much is clear. And some piece of me still wants him to
be happy.

When I reach my car, I wrench the door open and click
on my seatbelt. Then, I fix my appearance in the rearview
mirror.

She's not a slow mover because she has trust issues, I think,
trying to get my head on straight. *She's moving slow because
she's got someone else on the line. This mysterious 'W.' that sent
the roses.*

I will figure out who "—W" is. I'll record evidence that
Mike can't refute. And I know just the man to help me do it.

22

———

"THE ONE"

The churro shop was a curveball. My plan to bring my two targets closer may not have worked as I anticipated, but it still worked. Mike and Zoe have bonded over a failed date.

I watched as Cassandra tailed them. From the time she left her apartment, I followed her car, a flawed guardian making sure she is never alone. I parked across the street from the Churro shop, looking out my window as Cassandra stalked her prey. She was wearing that little sweatshirt, pulling the hoodie tight over head as if it made her less noticeable.

She has such a tiny frame. Cassandra is a waif of a thing. It hurt me to see her alone on the side-walk— all ninety pounds of her— thin like a reed waving on the planes. Cassandra doesn't carve her own path. She's so small she looks as if she's at risk of just disappearing one day. She allows herself to be carried from place to place, a woman in the wind, blown to each location by the forces of other people. I know she worries she's invisible. But she isn't.

You could never be invisible, I think. Not as long as I love you.

Mike is almost entirely out of the picture. Soon, he'll commit to this new woman, and Cassandra will have what she needs to let go. All thanks to me. We're closer than ever to being together. And when I see her tomorrow, somewhere deep inside, she'll feel it too.

23

CASSANDRA

If I can just get through this shift, I'll get to see Jerry. I'm thinking about him obsessively, but not because of any attraction to him— only because he can supply me with the necessary tech gear to catch Zoe in a recorded lie. Jerry and I have made plans to meet up after my shift at the home decor store, and it's the only thing on my mind. As I dust the display cases by the front door, I think about how it will feel to reveal Zoe as a fraud.

Maybe I'll catch video of footage of Zoe and "W" together in an intimate position, which I'll email to Mike from an anonymous account. When I'm ringing up yet another customer, I imagine Mike running into the store, telling me how lucky he is that he has someone like me looking out for him. Someone like me keeping him from making the biggest mistake of his life. I'm imaging the same scenario when I accidentally drop a decorative, ceramic bowl I was unpacking. It falls onto the floor with a horrible cracking noise, pieces scattering everywhere. Patricia clucks her tongue at me.

"Seriously?" She says, shaking her head. "What's wrong with you today?"

"Sorry," I sigh, heading to get the broom from the storage closet. Patricia surprises me by meeting me halfway with the dustpan.

"If I didn't know any better I'd say you had sex brain," she says, bending down to hold the dustpan into place.

"What?"

"You know," she elaborates. "The thing that happens to your brain after you've had a good lay. You start getting clumsy. Thinking about the person all the time. You're totally giving the vibe." She scans me up and down, her dark hair sticking up in a mohawk, one side of her head shaved down. Patricia would be intimidating if she didn't look so young.

"You caught me," I say, shrugging.

"Does he feel the same way about you?" She empties the dustpan into the trashcan.

"Definitely not," I tell her honestly.

"Well fuck that," she shakes her head. "Stop destroying my merchandise over some guy who doesn't give a shit about you. Pull it together, okay?"

"Fair enough. I'll work on it."

"You wanna come to listen to metal tonight?" She asks, barely making eye contact with me. Patricia despises me and only offers the occasional opportunity to hang out as a polite gesture she hopes I won't accept. "I go to a place in Marina del Ray every Thursday night. Sick venue in the back of a speakeasy. The noise'll clear your head so good you won't care if the idiot ever touches you again. It'll get your thoughts straight."

"Wow," I say. "That sounds really great, but I have plans."

Plans to bug my ex-boyfriend's new girlfriend's house, I think to myself.

"Your loss," she shrugs, sauntering away with the broom and the dustpan.

She's right. I need to pull it together. And the only way to screw my head on straight is to show Mike what a huge mistake he's making using whatever means necessary.

Even illegal ones.

AFTER MY SHIFT ENDS, I cross the shopping center and make my way to Jerry's store. He's managed to keep the interior sparkling fresh since we redecorated together. Everything is still organized in a visually pleasing fashion, and big signs overhead direct customers to the right areas. "Cameras." "Security Systems." "Personal Defense." It's all neatly labeled, nestled underneath a sign I had printed in tight, arial font. In the back, an accent wall painted a soothing robin's egg blue ties it all together. A seating area in the middle of the store allows customers to discuss their security needs in a calm atmosphere.

I take a seat on the couch, smiling at Jerry, who hasn't spotted me yet. He's in the back, stocking a shelf with battery-operated cameras.

"You haven't destroyed my art yet?" I call out. "I'm surprised. I thought for sure you'd have torn the place apart by now."

Jerry whirls over his shoulder, looking surprised, but happy to see me. "You're early," he says, checking a smart watch on his wrist. "I was planning to use the next ten minutes to create a mess."

"Terrible," I shake my head.

"Ah, not so terrible," he shrugs, dusting off his hands and taking the seat next to me on the couch. "Messing up the store would mean I'd have an excuse to ask you back."

My heart flutters in my chest a little. Every now and then, Jerry manages to stir a feeling inside me I haven't noticed since Mike left. It never lasts long— maybe be I actively try to squash it. If I fall for someone like Jerry, it means officially letting go of Mike. Such a thing would feel like grieving a death. I'm not read for it.

Still, he has such nice eyes. Flirting never hurt a person. "Maybe you don't need an excuse," I tell him.

"I'll keep that in mind," he agrees.

I clear my throat, getting down to business. "It's time for you to keep your end of the deal. I need spy gear. Lots of it. It's imperative the equipment be reliable, but that it can't be traced back to me if discovered."

"Dare I ask," he leans forward on the sofa, resting his elbows on his knees, "Who you're spying on?"

"I told you," I say, a little rattled. "My dog sitter."

"I meant the real story," Jerry pushes. "Not the bullshit lie you have me when we were strangers. Look," he throws his hands in the air like he means no harm. "All I know is you're never covered in dog hair..."

"Maybe I'm just really clean," I protest.

"Your screensaver is a blank clock and not a picture of your pet," he adds.

"Maybe I'm private!"

"Okay," Jerry nods. "Quick, what's your dogs name?"

"Fido." The obvious answer slips out before I can realize how stupid it was to pick the most cliche dog name in the world. Jerry gives me a knowing look. "Fido junior?" I try again.

Jerry laughs. "It's fine, you don't have to tell me," he

adds. "I know people have their reasons and it's none of my business. I just wanted you to know I'm a friend and you can trust me. If you need help and someone's scaring you, I'm here."

My heart beats a little more quickly in my chest. It's rare to find a person like Jerry. Someone who gives a fuck. Strangely, I don't want him to see me as weak. I want him to believe I'm the kind of person who can take care of myself.

"The truth is, it's not for me," I say. "Let's just say it's a friend of a friend."

"I'm not helping you engage in any unethical activities?" he asks. "I don't care about illegal, but unethical is another thing."

"I've got this friend, and I happen to know the girl he's seeing is going to hurt him," I say, deciding I can trust Jerry with at least half of the truth. "She's going to hurt him in a big, life-ruining way. But if I try to tell him without evidence, he likes her so much that he won't believe me. I need to catch her in the act to be able to prove it to him and stop him from making the biggest mistake of his life."

"I see," Jerry nods. "Is this friend *just* a friend?"

"Is that an official question you ask every customer?" I tease.

"Only the ones I'm hoping will get dinner with me tonight," Jerry says.

"Hook me up with cameras and we'll see about dinner," I smile.

"Fine," Jerry laughs. "You got me. Let's take a look at the goods." There's a pause as he scans me up and down. "Thanks for telling me the truth. I'm not sure I like the answer, but I know whatever you're doing— it's to help someone."

"How do you know that?" I ask.

"Because I'm a good judge of character."

He takes my hand and pulls me off the couch, leading me toward the camera section. "You need something undetectable," he says, motioning at shelf of different options. "If it's battery operated, you'll only get so much life out of it before the battery needs to be changed. How much access do you have to the place you're installing these?"

"Not nuch," I admit. "I might only get one go at it."

"Then you're going to want three things," Jerry says, counting the items off on his fingers. "Something that has long battery life, something that can remotely send you the recordings, and something that can go undetected." He reaches for a small, circular camera on the shelf, no bigger than the top of an ink pen. "I recommend these little guys." He holds the camera up on his fingertip, allowing me to examine the reflective, black glass. "You can stick them anywhere. There's adhesive on the back. They connect to your phone via an app, so you can always access the tapes. And they're small enough the battery life is pretty impressive. You should get at least three weeks out of 'em."

"What if it's discovered?" I say, suddenly nervous about the idea of connecting something to my phone. "Would the police be able to tell it's me?"

"Nope," Jerry shakes his head. "You can't reverse engineer 'em that way. Besides, there's a remote disconnect option. At any point you go into the app and ditch the camera. It won't store any information about where it's been connected."

"I'll take five," I laugh.

Jerry removes the cameras from the shelves, packing the little boxes into a basket for me. "Remember to stick them somewhere they blend in. People are used to looking around their homes and will notice if even the smallest thing stands out. The edges of the doorways are great. Potted plants. Picture frames. That sort of thing."

"Will do," I say. "What about audio?"

"There's a little speaker on the side." He reaches for the sample camera again and flips it over, revealing a small, netted hole that serves as a microphone. "It's not great but it'll do. If you have five in close range, you'll get audio on at least one, probably two. Just depends on how close the subject is."

"Perfect," I tell him. And it is. All I need to do is access Zoe's place again. Maybe I can sneak in tonight, or stake out her place and wait for her to leave to make another move.

"Dinner," Jerry says, like he knows what I'm thinking. "Before you go super spy, let's at least get some food you. It's on me."

I'm hesitant to agree. I don't like to let people close to me, because they might discover my favorite hobby: following Mike. Still, it doesn't hurt to have friends who understand you, and Jerry— in his own quiet kind of way— makes me feel understood. Mike's exploring other connections. Why shouldn't I?

"Dinner," I agree, and just like that, we're locking up the shop and walking down the mall to a little barbecue place on the edge of the strip.

24

"THE ONE"

Cassandra is careful during dinner. Careful not to say too much about herself. She keeps people at arms length, and I know why:

She fears being discovered. She doesn't want to be known. To be seen. The fear of having her own life reflected back at her through the perception of another person is too frightening a prospect.

Still, she leans in during the conversation. She even shares her side dish— a plate of baked beans. She allows the small barbecue restaurant— with its red-checkered table-clothes and cold, metal tables— to become a safe place for both of us. She is using this experience to show me she is ready for more than Mike. She is ready to let go.

This dinner is a performance, and it exists only to subtly signal to me that she is open for more. I can see it in the way she flips her hair. The way she smiles. It's all subconscious of course, but her entire being is asking to be pursued.

The fact that she even accepted the dinner invitation in the first place shows growth.

She is moving on from Mike. My efforts are working. We

have almost reached the moment I've been waiting for. The pinnacle of my plan— the moment in which I reveal myself to her and become more than just "the one," but a face, and a name.

We are so close.

25

CASSANDRA

I can't stop thinking about dinner with Jerry. I'm parked outside of Zoe's apartment, waiting for her to leave so I can install my cameras in secret. But as I stare up at her brick apartment building, my mind keeps flashing to moments from last night.

I'd been to the barbecue joint before. It's one of only a few restaurants in the mall where the home decor store is located, so it's a regular stop for me. But being there with Jerry felt different. Everything tasted a little better, maybe because I wasn't eating alone. Being with Jerry was easy. He told me why he got into home security.

"It was because of what happened," he said, motioning to the gash on his face. "I realized how dangerous the world could be, and I wanted to help other people protect themselves."

I took another bite of the baby-back ribs in front of me. "No offense, but selling to the wrong person could make the world more dangerous."

"I try to trust that most people are just doing the best with what's in front of them," Jerry shrugged. "Is it wrong to spy on someone? Sure. But maybe it's a woman who wants to know if her husband's cheating. Or a guy who worries he's being set up for a crime by an angry ex and wants video evidence to prove he didn't do anything wrong. Basically," Jerry continued. "I try to give people the benefit of the doubt."

"That's a bold strategy."

"Not one you're willing to try?" Jerry asked, taking another swig of his beer.

"I don't think it would work out well for me," I told him honestly. "Anytime I think I know someone and can trust them, they just end up disappointing me."

A pained looked flashed across Jerry's face, but I couldn't quite place what it meant. Then, he seemed to recover.

"What about you family?" Jerry asked. "Are any of them good people?"

"Yes," I told him. "But we don't talk anymore so it doesn't matter."

"You don't talk to your parents?" Jerry said, surprise coating his voice. "Why not?"

Because I am the biggest disappointment, I thought without saying it aloud. I knew I couldn't tell Jerry the truth: I haven't talked to my parents in ages because I know all I will ever do is let them down. They've tried to make me stay on medication that's supposed to help me, but I only stick to the regimen for a few weeks before flushing it down the toilet. My parents have tried to get me into every mental health program available, spending endless amounts of money to ensure my well-being, but I always flunk out. The problem is that they want me to be a certain kind of way— productive, normal, healthy— and they don't understand that I'm happier just accepting where I'm at. Their attempts to "fix" me just make me feel worse about myself.

I turned back to Jerry, unable to explain it all away. "We're not close," I said, pushing food around my plate with my fork. "They're always trying to fix me."

"Parents are like that," Jerry agreed. He reached into his pocket, pulling out his wallet and removing a photo that he passed across the table. "That's my son," he explained. I examined the picture, noting a little boy of about three with Jerry's eyes, sitting cross-legged in a sandbox. "I'd do anything to help him. It's just what parents do."

"I know," I answered.

"Things didn't work out with his Mom, but I'll always make sure I'm there for him. Try to cut your parents some slack," Jerry added, taking the photo out of my hand and putting it back in his wallet. "They're trying."

Now, as I sit outside Zoe's apartment, thinking about the fact that she's somebody's daughter— Jerry's words take on a fresh meaning. I shouldn't be here. I should be working on my own situation and accepting the help my parents have offered me. They don't even know my address. They don't know how to reach me because I changed my phone number months ago. And if they knew I was sitting outside a stranger's apartment, preparing to ruin a budding rela-tionship for my own benefit, they'd be disappointed. Even more so that I'm involving Jerry, who has a business and a child of his own— so much to lose if he's caught helping me in a criminal act.

I should stop. I should turn this car around and leave, never to return. My fingers close around the keys and I'm about to turn them over in the ignition when there's a banging sound from the apartment across the street. The front door slams shut behind a small but sturdy figure. It's Zoe. She's leaving.

The apartment is empty.

It's now or never. This is my chance. It's a small moment, but something about it feels like the kind of thing that could make or break a person. My eyes scan my car keys, still perched in the ignition, begging me to leave.

Instead, I rip them from the dashboard and shove them in my pocket. I grab my cell phone, opening "Contacts" and hitting Jerry's name, a thrill making my skin prickle when he picks up on the first ring.

"Hello?" his voice echoes out from the speaker. He's been waiting for my call. I told him I'd let him know when I was ready.

"We're good," I tell him. "I'll text you the address."

And just like that, I've done a terrible thing.

I ENTER the apartment the same way I did on my first intrusion, and it remembers me like an old friend. The door clicks open with ease, and the scent of Zoe's home hits me hard— it's a unique combination of gardenia and burned sage, combined with the faint edge of unclean clothes from the piles of laundry stacked on the floor. Sweat gathers on my forehead as I rush to hide picture frames in drawers in order to temporarily hide any trace of Zoe's identity. Jerry thinks this apartment belongs to both my male friend and his female love interest, not Zoe alone. I thought the lie would make the scenario more plausible. In Jerry's eyes, I'm helping a friend discover that his girlfriend is cheating on him before he proposes to her, making the biggest mistake of his life. At least, that's what I've let him believe. He probably suspects I have some feelings for the friend as well, but if he notices, he doesn't seem to mind.

When I'm certain I've hidden every picture frame, I scan the apartment one more time for any items that might reveal the way in which I've lied. Nothing appears, and— like clockwork— there's a faint knock at the door. When I open it, Jerry is standing on the other side, holding bags of technical equipment.

"Should we get to it?" he asks.

"Come on in," I tell him. He strides to the couch and drops the bags on its fluffy surface. "Sure your friend can be the girlfriend away for a few hours."

"He promised me," I said. "He took her on a surprise date to the zoo."

"So he's starting to come around, then?" Jerry asks, unpacking the remote cameras from their small boxes and lining them up in a row. They look like little soldiers, ready to do my bidding.

"He doesn't totally believe me, but he's starting to suspect something's not right," I lie. "Flowers came the other day and she explained them away, but he's coming around to the idea she could be having an affair."

"Painful stuff," Jerry nodded, and for the first time, I wonder why he's no longer in a relationship with the mother of his child. Jerry pauses, the final camera arranged in the line. He turns to me. "You're *sure* you want to do this?" The look in his eyes makes me pause. It's as if he's testing me, or trying to warn me.

"Yes," I tell him.

He shifts his weight from one leg to the other. "Once we do this there's no going back. You and your friend— you're going to know thing you might be better off not knowing."

"Are you speaking from personal experience?"

Jerry shakes his head. "I just know that sometimes if better to move on than to try to find out. Sometimes the right move is to let go." He stares at me when he says the final words, "let go," putting to much emphasize on both of them.

"I want to know," I repeat myself.

Disappointment flashes across his face, but he covers it quickly. "Should we get to it then?" He claps his hands together, suddenly all business. "We need to put one in each room. Two would be better." He passes me the tiny cameras and shows me the adhesive on the back, offering instructions as to where they're best placed. "You want to pick a spot where they'll blend in, but also think about what could go wrong. Here..." He motions at me and I follow him toward a potted plant in the corner. "See, this seems like a good idea, but people move their plants all the time, and if they overwater, the camera could get wet. A better spot is right over there..."

He leads me the sliding door that sits behind the potted plant. It's a glass slider— a standard feature on any apartment with a balcony— but the frame that holds in it place is solid black. "We can hide it on the metal ridge. People can move furniture, but they don't move built-in elements. Plus, when was the last time you looked at the edge of your window frame?"

"Never," I tell him, making a mental note to search my entire apartment for cameras from top to bottom when I get home.

"That's the thing," Jerry agrees. "Most people aren't looking on the edges. The fringes of life. That's where all the trouble is." He sticks the camera to the edge of the frame and it blends right in with the black paint. It looks like nothing more than an odd little magnet, no bigger than a dime.

"If I found that in my apartment, I wouldn't even know it was a camera," I confess.

"That's the idea," he agrees. "Let's tackle every room."

We take on the chore section by section, making sure there's a camera not just in the living room, but in each area of Zoe's apartment. In the kitchen, we strategically adhere the camera to a bolt on top of the fridge— it's a connective piece no one would look at twice. In the bedroom, we settle on hiding the camera on the corner of a bookshelf that's heavy and settled. It's the kind of furniture piece that stays in one place for a long time, and judging by the plethora of books on its shelves, Zoe isn't planning to move it anytime soon.

We stop in front of the bathroom door, glancing at each other.

"I generally advise against bathrooms," Jerry says, his voice tentative. "Something about it just seems too..."

"Wrong?" I finish his sentence for him.

"Yeah," he nods. "Besides, if you're trying to catch her in the act of cheating, you'll know as soon as the guy enters the front door. No need to go the distance."

He has a point. I think about it, and then decide that even *I* have limits. I'm already doing on wrong thing— might as well stop while I'm behind. "We skip the bathroom," I agree. Jerry pockets the last remaining camera, then pauses, an idea hitting.

"We could put the last camera in the hallway," he says. "You'd be surprised what people catch when they film hallways. Lotta weird stuff goes down."

Yeah, I think, *like me, creeping toward the apartment of my ex-boyfriend's new girlfriend.*

"Let's put one in the hallway," I agree, and we make our way out the front door. After some analysis, we decide the camera is best positioned above the door frame, at the edge where the wall meets the ceiling. Jerry gives me a boost on his shoulder, perching me there like a bird so I can reach. The camera sticks, he lets me down, and the job is done.

We go back inside, shutting the door softly behind us.

"Give me your phone," Jerry says, his arm outstretched. For a moment, I want to decline. A wave of nausea washes over me. Giving my phone to another person feels like a violation. Still, I need his help. And it's just Jerry. He's proven himself to be trustworthy. He's just helped me commit a crime, after all.

Reluctantly, I pass my phone to him. He glances up at me. "Unlock it?" I enter my passcode, and the screen makes a clicking noise as the phone unlocks.

Jerry opens the app store and downloads a specific program. The logo on the app is a single eye, wide-open, a magnifying glass laid over its iris. Jerry clicks on it, bringing me to the dashboard. He commits some act of wizardry, linking each camera to the program, then passes the phone back to me so I can see.

Multiple square boxes project Zoe's living room back at me, each of them providing a different view of her apartment.

"See?" Jerry points at the phone. He singles out a box that features him and me, standing shoulder-to-shoulder. He waves in the air, and his video-self waves back on the screen. "It's almost in real-time. Barely a one-second delay. And it auto records anytime there's motion. So you can go back and watch any videos you missed."

"This is amazing," I say. "I can't thank you enough. I hope we catch her."

"Nothing worse than a cheater," Jerry answers. "Glad I could help."

"We should…"

"Definitely."

Jerry helps me erase any trace of our presence. He straightens the pillows, and makes sure none of the furniture we examined has been moved out of order. I grab the packaging for the cameras and throw it in the trash.

"Don't you think that's a giveaway?" Jerry asks, a smile tugging at the corner of his mouth.

"Oh my gosh," I say, not able to believe my own stupidity. I reach into the trashcan and remove the packaging, but something else catches my eye. A discarded letter, and an envelope beside it, with a simple letter "W." hand-written on the front.

Zoe got another note from "W.." I think, unable to contain my excitement. I leave the letter in the trash to as not to tip Jerry off, then pass him the remains of the camera boxes.

"Thanks again," I say.

"Sure you don't want to leave with me?"

"My friend said he's taking her to Mom's place, so he's coming alone. I just want to show him what we did," I claim.

"And this guy is really just a friend, huh?"

"Yes," I say.

"Must be a pretty good one," Jerry starts to leave, then pauses. "Hope this doesn't mean I won't see you around the store anymore."

"Something tells me you won't be able to get rid of me," I smile at him. "Besides, I'm pretty sure you're the kind of guy who can find me anytime you like." I point at the location of the camera in the living room.

"Don't be a stranger," he says. Then shuts the door

behind him. I wait until his footsteps have disappeared, then double-check the hallway camera on my new spy app. The hallway is empty. I'm finally alone.

As quickly as possible, I run through Zoe's apartment and remove all the picture frames from the drawers in which I hid them. With painstaking effort, I arrange them in their original positions.

When the job is done, my legs carry me toward the trash and I reach inside, pulling out the ripped envelope marked *W.*, along with the letter that rests next to it.

My hands shake, and I'm desperate to read the letter in the apartment. But I know I have to leave— Zoe could come back at any moment. The letter will have to wait until I get home.

Home.

I smile to myself, thinking about how strange it is that I have two homes, now. My own lousy apartment in Van Nuys, and Zoe's apartment, which I can access from the little digital world inside my phone.

Congrats, Zoe, I think. *You've got yourself a new roommate.*

26

"THE ONE"

She isn't ready to let go.

Cassandra could have spent her day doing one of a hundred beneficial activities. She could have gone to the park. She could have created a plan for her life— maybe looked into school, and considered getting a new advanced degree in something more useful than design. She could have gone on a date. Maybe even a date with me.

Instead, she chose to spend her time installing cameras in Zoe's apartment. She was offered the choice to walk away. I watched her fumbling the keys in car, thinking about leaving. But instead, she chose to dedicate herself to someone who isn't me. Again. Even when I'm right in front of her.

She has so much potential. She could achieve so many things with that curious mind of hers. I've seen it in action myself. I've watched her as she's designed a space, figuring out every angle. Seizing every opportunity to create beauty. But she insists on hiding herself in the life of another person.

Suddenly, I feel jealous of Zoe. I know Cassandra's interest in her isn't romantic, but still— Zoe gets Cassandra's attention. Her time. Her focus. I am nothing but a supporting character in her story. And despite my best efforts, she still doesn't see me as "the one."

I didn't want to do this, but I will have to take things to the next level. Cassandra has left me with no choice. I gave her the time and space to make up her own mind. I've been patient.

But now, we've reached an impasse. A moment of reckoning. I'm going to force Cassandra to confront her weaknesses by removing the people who mislead her.

I'm going to take the one person who distracts her from me, and force her to look my way. When I take the one who manipulates her focus, she will be forced to acknowledge me.

She will see that I'm "the one."

27

CASSANDRA

The letter from *W.* only left me with more questions. It was simple— handwritten— scrawled on the inside of a card that had a picture on the front of a Husky dog sitting beside a heart balloon. When I opened the card up, the typed message from the card company read "I *woof* you very much." On the opposite side, the note from *W.* said, simply, "It's late. But is it ever too late? Please let me try again."

She's broken it off with him and he's trying to get back into her good graces, I thought as I tossed the card in the garbage can, discouraged. To make Mike break up with Zoe, I'd need hard evidence that she couldn't be trusted. A jilted ex-lover wouldn't be enough. Still, I hoped the cameras would give me something more.

And that's the good news. There's a new hobby in my life, and I almost like it better than following Mike. Every day, I watch Zoe on the cameras. The app Jerry installed on my phone is— to me— what instagram, or twitter is to others. It's a compulsion. Something I can't help but open. My subconscious mind pulls my fingers toward the app without active thought, and before I know it, I'm spying on Zoe again.

There's something intimate about knowing her this way. Her daily routines have become *my* daily routines. Her morning activities are familiar to me now, and she performs them like a ritual, down to the minute. She wakes up. Hits "snooze" once. Wakes up again. Puts on pajamas. It's interesting to me— as a fellow woman— that Zoe sleeps naked, but bothers to put on pajamas when she wakes up even when she lives alone. I do the same thing, but now that I see it on camera, I wonder why anyone who lives alone bothers to wear clothes at all. *Who are we hiding from?*

After putting on her pajamas, Zoe heads for the kitchen, and makes herself a modest breakfast. She's not a world class chef. In fact, her meals are sadder than my own. A single banana. A cup of yogurt. Sometimes if she's feeling really ambitious, she even pours milk over a bowl of dry granola. In the days I've been watching her, I've never once seen the woman scramble an egg. *What a pathetic wife she'd make for Mike,* I think to myself. At least when he lived with me, he'd get the occasional cooked chicken or meatloaf.

Once she's indulged her pitiful breakfast, Zoe leaves, presumably to go to work at the hotel. She appears to work long hours, and gets home late— long past the typical hours of a nine-to-five job. In the three days I've been watching her, she's had one date with Mike. They went to see a movie together, and made out in the car after, but she didn't invite back to her apartment. On the nights she's been alone, she takes a long bath, calls her Mom on the phone and talks for hours about nothing, checks her emails at her desks, and falls asleep to the National Geographic Channel.

Taking it all as a whole, I'm almost a little disappointed in how boring Zoe appears to be. If I'm going to lose Mike to another woman, I'd at least like her to be worldly or interesting. It strikes me that maybe Mike traded down. Sure, I may have my flaws— I'm aware of the chaos I create, and the flames I fan. But at least I'm creative— a passionate dreamer with an eye for beauty. At least I'm not boring.

For three days, I've endured watching Zoe's mediocre life unfold within the undecorated walls of her average, grey box of an apartment. I've waited eagerly for any sign of the mysterious man named *W.* but her hasn't come.

Begrudgingly, I tuck my phone away and head to the Home Decor store for yet another day of meaningless, vapid work. It's an hour before store opening and I'm tying my apron on when Patricia finds me and tasks me with creating a display for our newest inventory. "It's the hottest new trend," she says, the tone of her voice saying she only cares about the money to be made and not whatever kitschy knick-knacks are hot at the moment.

She pushes a cardboard box in front of me, its lid wide open. Disgust bubbles in my stomach as I peek inside, staring at a collection of animal-themed glassware. Mugs with hand-painted cats on their curved faces. Plates with tiny dogs playing fetch, their legs running around the circumference of each. Salad bowls with hamsters decorating the rim.

"I don't know what to do with this," I tell her honestly. "If this is the newest trend I just— I can't—"

"Me too," she agrees. She smiles at me. This might be the first time I've ever seen Patricia smile. Her teeth are alarmingly straight, and too white when juxtaposed against her dyed, dark hair. The piercing in her nose floats above them like a stud in a tiara. "I didn't know what to do with it either and that's why I'm giving it you instead."

"Lucky me," I tell her.

"Hey," she shrugs. "You have a talent for design. If anyone can make it work, it's you."

"Thanks," I say, mildly surprised at the compliment. "That was actually really nice." I'm surprised. This isn't the Patricia I know.

She snorts. "Well, I mean, we didn't hire you for your looks or personality, so at least you the one thing you do have."

There she is, I think, nodding at the version of Patricia I'm used to.

Without another complaint, I slide the box toward an empty display on the back wall, emptying its contents onto the floor in neat little rows. My hands busy themselves, trying to arrange the display into something pleasing on the eye. I retreat to the storeroom temporarily and come back with a pushcart filled to the brim with greenery— fake flowers, artificial green ferns— all of which will be used to soften the blow of animal glassware.

In-between wondering what kind of person can pay thirty dollars for a single, hand-painted cat pitcher, I think about Zoe. Based on the time of day, she's probably just wrapping up her morning routine. She gets into the hotel around 9 a.m. on Wednesdays, and a quick glance at the clock on the wall tells me it's only 7:15 a.m. If I could find a moment to glance at my phone, I could see her again.

I'm not supposed to use my phone at work, but everyone's entitled to a break. A quick glance over my shoulder tells me Patricia has disappeared— she's probably enjoying her vape pen in the back alley where the trash cans are stored. She's a smoker, which is a gift to us all because it means she has a habit of disappearing for extended periods of time.

This might be my only chance for awhile, I think, pulling

my phone out of my pocket. My legs groan as I sink onto a nearby display sofa, eagerly tapping the screen like an addict getting a hit. The app opens, and an image of Zoe's living room appears before me like a village in a snow globe — a tiny world I can access from the palm of my hand.

Zoe appears in the center of the screen, a figurine in the tableau I've created. She's pacing across the kitchen floor. There's a cup of yogurt on the table but she hasn't touched it. One hand holds her phone up to her ear, and the other gestures wildly. Whoever she's talking to is on the receiving end of a rant. It's hard to tell from the camera's low resolution, but it looks like her eyes are crinkled— I think she's *crying.*

My heart pounds as I lean in, turning up the phone's volume. Zoe's voice echoes through the speakers.

"You left me—" she says, her voice cracking. "You can't just come back now and try to make it right."

She turns, stopping at a bouquet of roses on the entryway table. They're in a plastic vase, and one of those tiny balloons beloved by flower delivery services has been clipped to the vase's edge.

Those weren't there last night, I think, zooming in on the video to get a closer look at the flowers. *He sent her flowers again.* My brain whirls, trying to make sense of the situation. There's only one conclusion: *She's on the phone with W.*

"Yes, they're beautiful," Zoe says, reaching out for the flowers. She touches one of the petals, sliding it between her fingers. "I just have a lot going on right now..."

She pauses, listening to the person on the other end. *W.* must be pleading his case. Zoe slumps into a chair, phone still up to her ear.

"How do I know it will be different this time?" she asks, waiting for his response. There's a long pause as she listens.

Then, finally, she says, "Yes. I know it's just a meal. Fine. Dinner. But I need it to be a place I know…"

She's going to meet with him, I think, my heart racing at the idea of finally putting a face to the name. *She's going to give W. a chance to win her back, even while she's dating Mike.*

This is the evidence I've needed. One simple viewing of the video makes it clear— Zoe has other suitors. I could wait until the meeting between Zoe and W., but by then, Mike might be so in love with her he doesn't care about the problems staring him right in the face. Mike gets carried away when it comes to matters of the heart. The fact he dated me so long is proof enough of that.

My fingers shake as I save the video file to my phone, moving to open my email account. I've already created an anonymous account through a proxy site that blocks the IP address of the sender. I made it days ago just in case something liked this happened.

I open a new email, the upload the video as an attachment. In the recipient field, I type in Mike's work email address, which I know by heart. The subject line gives me pause, but after thinking for a minute, I type in the simple message: *Zoe isn't who you think she is.* In the body of the email, I simply type *"from a friend."* Mike may eventually realize this email is from me, considering he's caught me following him multiple times, and has gone to great efforts to conceal his whereabouts. But I need to grab him from the start so he at least watches the video— and with a subject line like that, who could resist?

My thumb hovers over the little airplane icon that indicates a "send" command. For a second, I wonder if this is another opportunity to turn around— to change course. I think about Jerry, and how kind is. I like the way he doesn't ask too many questions, and how he makes me feel like the best version of myself. But I'm still not ready to let go of Mike. Jerry is a distraction. He's not the ultimate goal.

There's a whooshing sound as I hit the little icon, causing the email to send.

It's done. In a few short hours or less, Mike will know who he's really dating. He'll have irrefutable evidence that Zoe can't be trusted.

For celebration's sake, I open up the video again, watching as Zoe paces, cell phone in hand. But before I can enjoy the accomplishment, the sound of a throat clearing echoes behind me. I whirl around, finding Patricia, who is positively *seething*.

"What did I tell you about using phones at work?"

You told me you'd fire me on the spot, I think. The last time Patricia caught me sending a simple text message at work, she reacted like a jealous lover and demanded to know who could possibly be so important. She made it clear usage of phones was a fireable offense. One I've continued to commit behind her back whenever possible.

"Sorry about that," I say, dropping the phone into my apron pocket.

"Are you watching porn?" she says, her voice low. "That girl in the apartment... is that an OnlyFans feed?"

It takes me a second to realize what she's talking about. She thinks Zoe is a paid internet performer, and I'm a voyeur, getting my jollies in exchange for cash.

"No, she's..." I start to defend myself but quickly realize there's no good explanation for why I'm watching a woman walk around her apartment.

"That's what I thought," Patricia nods. She steps forward and gets too close to my face so she's almost nose-to-nose with me. "Do you know how pathetic that is?" She practically spits the words at me. "There are real women all around you who you could actually ask out, but instead you waste your time on a fucking app?"

"Um," I say. "It's not like that..."

She points at me, her lips in a snarl. "Do you know how hard my family worked to build this business? And instead of working, you're chasing someone who doesn't even *want* you. Isn't that right?"

"I mean, kind of..." I admit. She's not wrong. Mike definitely doesn't want me. She's just mixed up about who I'm chasing. "This is actually a really funny misunderstanding."

"It'll be funnier when you check is docked," she takes a step back and crosses her arms. "No more work today. You don't need the hours."

"Excuse me?" I say, shocked she's cutting my shift back.

"Hurts, doesn't it?" She shakes her head. "I'll call you when we need you. Might be a few days though. But at least we give enough of a shit to reach out to you. Which is more than I can say for that stranger on the internet," she nods at the pocket of my apron, then strides off, her Doc Marten boots pounding against the floor.

Great, I think, wondering what I should do with myself for the rest of the day. I'm not just out the cash, but out the plans. Working at the store fills my time.

Still, it was worth it. I finally can show Mike he's making a terrible decision.

And— suddenly— I realize there's only on person I want to celebrate with.

28

"THE ONE"

Cassandra only falls deeper.

Deeper into her trauma. Deeper into self-sabotage.

She's lost wages. Been let go from work early. She's wandering around the mall like a lost puppy, her red apron curled up in her hand, trying to decide where to go— what to do with herself. She is lost, today, all because of the ones she follows when she should be running to me.

What will it take for her to come to me?

Will I have to wait until she's destroyed her meager life? Until she has no one else to turn to, and no one else to ask for comfort?

If that's the way it has to be— fine. I'll wait. I'll wait for her to see that Mike and Zoe are nothing but a distraction.

I'll wait for her to see that no one will ever be there for her like I will.

I'll wait for her to come to me. But it may take a push. And I know just what to do.

29

CASSANDRA

After walking around the mall for a bit, I stop at the frozen yogurt shop, grabbing two plain tarts and loading them up with every topping imaginable. The bill is a painful shock, but I don't care. Today is a day to celebrate.

Once I'm sure the lids are tightly affixed to the cups, I make my way to Jerry's shop, a giant grin plastered on my face.

"Well aren't you a sight for sore eyes," he says, opening the door to let me in.

"You busy today?" I ask him.

"Mornings are always slow," he answers, shaking his head. "And I'm never too busy for you."

He looks pleased as I hold out a frozen yogurt, offering it to him.

"It's a thank you for helping me with the cameras," I tell him.

"But the cameras were a thank you for you helping me with the store," he says as he sits down. "So after I eat this, I'll have give you a thank you for your thank you."

"I like where we're going with this," I agree, pulling the

spoon out of my mouth and letting the sweet chocolate chip topping melt in my mouth. We sit on the couches, and I'm relieved the store is empty today. It's like our own private house.

"It worked, didn't it?" Jerry says, clocking my blissful expression.

"We got her," I say, unable to keep myself from smiling. "She's exactly who I thought she was, and soon Mike's 'gonna know all about it. He won't be able to deny the video evidence."

Jerry shuffles a little on the couch next to me. Suddenly I realize how close we're sitting. "That's bad news for me then, huh?" He says. "This guy— you're old 'friend'— he'll be available and you won't care to see me quite as much."

"That's not true!" I exclaim. He looks at me out of the corner of his eye, dubious.

"You like him as more than a friend," Jerry says.

"Sure," I admit. "But that doesn't mean I won't want to see you. You're..." I pause, trying to find the right words. "You're the best thing that's happened to me in a long time."

"I can live with that," he says. He reaches forward, placing a hand on my cheek. And then— before I even realize what's happening— he leans in and kisses me. The feeling takes me by surprise. I haven't kissed anyone in awhile. But it's warm, and easy, and there's something so unassuming about it that I don't want it to stop. Jerry seems to take me exactly as I am. He doesn't expect too much of me, and seems happy with what he gets. Being around him isn't a tidal wave of passion, but more like a slow, easy burn. It's a little flame I want to pour fuel on, because it seems like it could grow.

We separate, and I stare at him for a minute, not sure what to say.

"Doesn't have to mean too much if you don't want it to," Jerry says, his voice quieter than a whisper. "I shouldn't have overstepped..."

Before he can apologize, I kiss him again. Longer this time, and with more passion. I what's left of my frozen yogurt fall on the floor, because I am like this. I am crazy, and wild, and free, and Mike never appreciated that I wasn't a thing to be counted on, but Jerry— Jerry seems to be fine with whatever I'm able to bring. But still— Mike was my forever, and I can't imagine we won't find our way back to each other. Especially now.

"I can't let go of him," I say, under my breath, and more to myself than to Jerry. "I'm just not ready."

"Hey," Jerry tucks my hair behind my ear, looking at me like I'm something rare. "That's okay. I'm not asking you to let go of anyone. Maybe just make some room for me and let's see where that takes us."

Then, we're kissing again, and my clothes are coming off, and I don't even care that the door to the store is unlocked. Anyone could come in and see us, but it doesn't matter. Because, for the first time in a long time— I'm not thinking about Mike.

BY THE TIME I get home, I'm on cloud nine. Today has been the best day I've had in awhile, on multiple fronts. My keys make a clanging noise as I toss them on the table and head straight for the refrigerator door. My stomach growls as I search for something to eat, finally pulling out a package of sliced cheese and some deli meat.

I sit on the couch, wrapping the cheese inside the meat and eating it without any bread like my own little *hors d'oeuvre.* The snack is satisfying, but I still feel like something is missing.

It's Zoe.

I'm so used to watching her on the cameras whenever possible— including mealtimes— that eating without her seems empty.

No reason I can't check in, I think.

I pull out my phone and open up the app. At first, everything looks normal in the bedroom, but when I switch to the live-feed of the living room, my stomach turns. My appetite disappears. Something is very wrong.

Zoe isn't alone in the living room anymore. Mike is in her apartment. For the first time ever.

This wasn't supposed to bring them closer, I think. It was supposed to drive them apart. My lungs expand as I take a deep breath in, trying to control my breathing. Maybe Mike's there because he's breaking up with her in person. He didn't give me much consideration when he ended our relationship, but it's possible he's learned from his mistakes and has decided to try and exit this connection with more grace.

Urgently, I turn up the volume using the buttons on the side of my phone, hitting a speaker icon so the sound from the video blares at me.

"But it means she's watching you..." Mike says loudly. He's pacing around the living room with such fervor I'm surprised he hasn't burned a hole in the carpet. "It *has* to be her. Who else would be motivated to do something like this? I should have told you sooner."

"There's never an easy time to tell someone you have a stalker," Zoe says, her voice quiet. She's sitting at the kitchen table, eerily calm, her arms folded in front of her.

"She's determined to ruin my life," Mike almost tears at

his hair. *Be careful,* I think. Mike is coming up on that age where hair is a lucky thing to have. Better not to tempt fate. "Cassandra just can't let go."

My cheeks flush, and I'm almost pleased to be included in this little moment between them. I haven't heard Mike say my name in a long time. It feels nice to be acknowledged.

Mike stops in his tracks. "The video," he says, looking around the room. "She could be watching us now."

Finally caught on, have you Mike?

He pulls out his phone and show the screen to Zoe, presumably playing the video I sent to his email inbox. They look around the room, trying to figure out the location of the source camera. Then, Mike walks toward the living room sliding door and feels around the edge of the frame.

Uh-oh.

His face fills the screen, and he's looking up at the sliding door, a curious expression on his face. He reaches up and pulls the tiny camera down. Now, it's settled in his hand, looking up into his nose.

Gross, but also a bummer.

"What are you gonna do with it?" I hear Zoe shout from the other room. There's a jostling moment as Mike walks away, and then a toilet comes into frame. The video goes flying. Mike tosses the camera into the toilet, and all I can see is water before the screen turns to static.

No problem. They've destroyed one camera. But I have others.

I switch to the kitchen view, looking through the lens of the camera on the edge of the fridge.

"We need to see if there's any others," Mike prompts Zoe to help him. The two of them get up and search the place, tearing Zoe's apartment up from top to bottom. The entire process takes about thirty minutes, and by the time they're done, they've completely swept the bedroom, and found every single camera I planted except two:

The camera in the hallway, and the camera on top of the fridge.

I'm pleased with this result. I can still see Zoe coming and going. Can still check on her at night from my perched position, aloft in the kitchen. Jerry was right when he said it's good to have backups.

Thinking they've secured the place, Zoe and Mike sit at the kitchen table, arms folded. Mike is a mess— sweating and breathing heavily. The stress of it all shows prominently in his hunched posture. In contrast, Zoe seems placid. Unmoved. She's *too* calm. It's unnerving.

"I think we got 'em all," Mike breaks the silence.

Think again. I take a sip of my soda.

"This means she was in my apartment," Zoe says slowly, like she's just piecing everything together. "I mean, *obviously* she was. It's just— strange to think about. Someone was in my apartment and I didn't even know."

"I shouldn't have dragged you into this," Mike says. "I understand if you don't want to see me anymore. I just wish— I mean, I hope you'll give me a chance to make it right."

Is he apologizing to her? My mouth drops open. He should be breaking up with her. *She's cheating on you!* I want to throw my phone through a window, but instead I hold it closer, staring intently at the screen.

"This isn't your fault," she says, her voice soft. She reaches across the table and puts her hand over his like she's trying to comfort him. "You didn't ask for this."

"But it's here anyway," Mike says. There's a pause as he considers. "And since it's here anyway— what was in the video— the phone call you took. I know it's not my business and I have no right to know..."

"True," Zoe says, a little harsher.

"But now that I *do* know, I can't exactly pretend it away" Mike continues. "Are you dating someone else? It's okay, if you are, I mean... we haven't had that conversation yet..."

"Dating someone?" Zoe blinks as if the idea never occurred to her.

"Well, yeah," Mike states the obvious. "The flowers. The phone call. You agreed to dinner..."

"That's not a date," Zoe says, running a hand through her hair. "You know how I said my Dad isn't around?"

Mike nods.

"He's come back. I haven't talked to him in years but he wants to reconnect. He got my address from my Mom. That's what the flowers were about. I keep telling him I'm not interested but I guess— when I was younger and he left he was in a different place. Now that he's aging he wants a connection. That's why he wanted to go to dinner. He keeps sending me cards with just his first initial on them— *W.* for William."

The cards are from her Dad? I think, my heart sinking. This won't make Mike break up with her. This new information will only make Mike like Zoe even more, because he has his own fucked up family. He'll relate.

"This is a mess," Mike puts his head in his hands. "I have no right to know this about you so early. You would've told me if you wanted me to know."

"I'm telling you now," Zoe shrugs. "The bigger question is, how far does this go?"

"What do you mean?" Mike looks up, confused.

Zoe speaks slowly, like she's piecing together a puzzle. "I

though it was so *odd* when you won that chamber of commerce of prize."

"Why?"

"Because all of the places on the list happened to be *my* favorite places. That Italian Restaurant. The ice cream shop. What are the odds you'd win a contest that took us to places I like? To be honest, I kind of assumed you were lying about the contest and had just looked me up on Facebook and picked all the locations I check into the most. I thought you were making up an excuse because you were trying to impress and you were shy or nervous or something."

"What?!" Mike laughs. "No! I would've just asked you where you wanted to go." He thinks for a second, bothered by something. "You know, I think you're onto something because..."

"What?" Zoe nods, eager to get to the bottom of the mystery in front of her.

"Well, I didn't even remember entering a contest when I got the email saying I'd won. I figured someone else put me in, or I was just having a lucky week between that and the dog shelter..."

"The dog shelter?" Zoe's ears perk up at the mention of their first date.

"Yeah," Mike nods. "They gave me that volunteer award. I didn't even know there *was* one."

"Because there isn't," Zoe stands, pacing around the kitchen. "There was no Chamber of Commerce contest. There wasn't a shelter volunteer award. And I bet if you asked the guy at the front desk he'd tell you someone paid him to make a big scene that day." She stops in her tracks. "But why? You said Cassandra doesn't want you to date anyone else..."

"She doesn't accept our breakup," Mike agrees. "In her mind, we're still together."

"Then *why* would she do all things that make you look good to me. It's like she *wants* us to be together."

Mike looks like he might throw up. He takes a deep breath, then stands and puts his hands on both of her arms, holding her like she's something precious. "Look, I can't explain crazy. I can't tell you why she's meddling except maybe it makes her feel like she matters. But I can promise you I'll keep you safe. Give me a chance to make to this right. I have her parents' number. I'll call them. I'll call the police. I'll do anything— to keep seeing you."

I've had enough. There's a clicking sound as I lock my phone screen, tossing it across the room with a forceful throw. It hits the wall then lands on the carpet, out of sight.

He still wants to be with her. But that's not the most troubling part of it all. Mike thinks I helped him win some contest, or that I meddled at the dog shelter. Why would I ever *want* him to date another woman? What I *want* is for to come back to me. To see that we belong together.

In fact, there's nobody I can think of that would meddle in such a way. What kind of person *would* want Mike to date Zoe so badly that they went to great lengths to promote the connection? It can't be someone else— besides me— who's obsessed with either one of them, because such a person would never benefit from creating a new relationship with the object of their affection. They'd want to destroy the relationship, just like I did. There's no reason to want Mike with Zoe, unless...

The idea hits me out of nowhere. There's no reason for someone to want Mike with Zoe, unless, for that person... it means Mike wouldn't be able to be with someone else. And the only other interested party pursuing Mike—

Is *me.*

Is it possible? Is it possible that someone has been trying to help Mike and Zoe get together in order to make me abandon all hope of us reconnecting?

Is there someone that follows me the way I follow Mike? For a moment, I consider the possibility that I'm just being paranoid, but the more I turn the idea over in my head, the more the pieces fall into place.

I've come home to find my front door unlocked multiple times in the last few months. But I always assume it's because I wasn't thinking and forgot to lock it, or was rushing off to follow Mike and let it go. But what if someone's been toying with the lock?

I've noticed the same Chevy parked on the street outside my house on weekends, and later noticed the same car behind me on my way to follow Mike. It's a distinct car — an old body style in a unique beige color— but I never thought too much about seeing it every now and then. I just assumed classic cars were making a comeback, or that a neighbor liked to go to the same places as me.

I never put it all together, because I *know* that I'm a little "off," a little different than everyone else, and I just assumed I was being paranoid. I assumed I couldn't trust myself.

But it's time to start now. I'm convinced of it: while I was trying to break Mike and Zoe up, someone else was trying to get to get them together. Because of me.

Because that person— is stalking me.

I leap up from the couch and grab my keys off the table. A quick search of the floor helps me find my cell phone— it's fallen behind an artificial plant in the corner. Two seconds later and I'm headed out the door to the one person I know can help me.

30

"THE ONE"

She will come to me, now.

Cassandra will have no choice. There is no more waiting. No more patience.

I've done everything I can to allow her to make her own choice, in her own time. But I've reached the limit.

When she sees what I've done, the tables will turn. I won't chase Cassandra anymore. She will come to me, because she will have to. And when she does, she'll understand what she's put me through. And together, we will make it right.

31

CASSANDRA

It's dark outside by the time I get to Jerry's shop. The shape of the outdoor strip mall creates a wind tunnel, and an evening gust blows through the strip. I pull my jacket tighter around my shoulders, hoping Jerry hasn't closed up yet for the evening. The Home Decor store I work at only stays open until 6p.m., but Jerry's hours run a little later due to the nature of what he sells. On most Friday nights, he's open until 8p.m.

The mall is quiet, devoid of foot-traffic— most patrons this time of night are headed straight for the movie theatre at the end of the block, and use our sad, little mall only as a place to steal free parking.

My legs carry me to Jerry's shop, and I stop at the front door. The sign on the front reads "OPEN," and a bell clangs as I enter.

"Jerry?"

No response. I'm surprised that there's no lights on in the store. It takes my eyes a minute to adjust to the darkness. Then, I see it:

Red drops on the rug. The rug that I helped Jerry choose when we redecorate the space.

My heart pounds as I bend down to examine the droplets more closely:

Blood.

"Jerry?!" I shout again, but no one answers. My body shakes as I follow the drops of blood to the back of the store. A display case of equipment has been toppled over, the contents spilled across the floor, cameras and listening devices in shambles. Their digital pieces lay uncased and revealed in front of me, impossible to repair. There was a struggle here, and judging by the blood, somebody lost. I hope it wasn't Jerry.

Finally, I make it to the back checkout counter, where Jerry usually rings up transactions. A smear of blood on the counter tells me this was where the fight happened. Judging by the blood spots, someone attacked Jerry back here, then drug him out the front door.

"Jerry," I whisper his name again, this time knowing for sure he won't answer me back. I take out my phone and turn the built-in flashlight on, using it to light up the space. For the first time, I notice a folded piece of paper on the counter. My name is written on it, in bold, typed letters.

"Cassandra."

The page crinkles as I unfold it and begin to read. It says, simply, "Meet me at your store." On the signature line, wet, blue ink spells out a name in hurried writing.

— Jerry.

32

"THE ONE"

I'm perched at the window of the Home Decor store, out of view behind a rack of dish-ware. My body hunches as I try to make myself smaller, staring out the glass at the empty strip mall outside. My eyes lock on to the doors of the security store, which I witnessed Cassandra enter only moments ago. Finally, the moment I've been waiting for arrives:

The doors to the security store burst open, revealing Cassandra, a storm across her face.

She's in plain view across the shopping center, but she doesn't know I'm here.

Her little body crosses the mall's walkway, full of intent. She's heading straight for the Home Decor store. Straight for me, just as I planned it.

She's beautiful when she's angry.

I've waited for this moment for so long. Now we can finally be honest with each other. We've grown closer, yes, but not close enough. Every time we're around one another, there's a level of deception. An element of subterfuge. Now, we can be honest with each other.

Tonight, I will tell her the whole truth.

And she will come to know me as who I really am. She will finally see me— as the one.

33

CASSANDRA

A bell dings as I open the doors to the Home Decor store. I've heard that bell ring a thousand times, but tonight it sounds ominous. It's announcing my presence with a kind of finality. There's no going back now. I'm here, and I'm looking for a fight.

The lights are off and my eyes take a moment to adjust. As the familiar space solidifies, it looks as it always does, except for one thing-- a trail of blood crossing the room. It leads toward the double doors the connect to our warehouse. I head for the doors, noting the EMPLOYEES ONLY sign on the front. We keep customers out of the warehouse because it isn't pretty.

A chill makes the hair on my arms stand up as the doors whip open, revealing the storeroom. It's an epic warehouse that rivals big competitors like Ikea, its sprawling cement footprint big enough to house couches and credenza. Overhead, exposed rafters reveal air conditioning tubes and electrical wiring. I've seen more than one rat scurry across the steel beams.

In the center of the warehouse, cardboard boxes fill the

floor-- someone has pushed all of our shipments into a single, central area. I can't imagine the work it took to move so many boxes into place. Nearby, I notice an abandoned forklift. Whoever did this must have used it— a union-only job, usually. The boxes are stacked so high I can't see over the top, and their formation reminds of something, although I can't place what it is. My hand shakes as I reach out to touch one, attempting to push it over. It doesn't budge— the inventory within is too heavy.

There's a crackling sound as a voice comes over the loudspeaker system we use to make announcements to customers. It's rigged to the warehouse so that employees working in the back can hear the calls as well.

"Meet me in the middle," the familiar voice says.

My feet freeze in place. *Jerry?* I think. The loudspeaker adds a sharp undertone to his voice, but the unmistakable baritone undoubtedly belongs to Jerry.

"Jerry!" I shout, my brain still trying to piece together some impossible puzzle. There's an answer licking at the edges of my mind, but it's not one I'm ready to hear. "Are you okay?"

"If you want to know the truth," he answers over the speaker system, "Find me in the maze."

Suddenly, it hits me. *The truth.* It couldn't be.

Has Jerry been stalking me? All this time I thought I could trust him. I saw him as a person I could let in on my darkest secrets-- someone who could help me achieve my deepest goal of wining Mike's attention again. Is it possible that— while I thought Jerry was helping me spy on Mike and Zoe— he was actually working behind my back to bring them together?

Has Jerry been following me?

"Why?" I say, surprised at the way my voice shakes. "Why are you doing this?"

I wait, but no answer comes. The loudspeaker system remains silent, leaving me in a haze. I step forward, looking at boxes in front of me. Suddenly, I know what they remind me of. They're arranged in the shape of a maze.

If I want the truth, there's no direction to go-- but forward. My legs carry me through an entrance created by boxes stacked in an arch. More boxes create a narrow corridor, and as I turn a corner, it hits me that I've been summoned into a Labrynth. Carboard walls create the limits. A quick left turn takes me to a dead end. There's a crackling sound as the loud speaker comes on and Jerry speaks through the overhead system.

"Wrong choice," his voice echoes in the space, omniscient and reaching.

He can see me, I realize. My eyes scan the maze, looking for any sign of a camera-- and then, I see it. A blinking red lit from the upper corner of the dead end where two boxes meet. The red light is attached to a square, lightweight camera that I remember seeing at the security store when I helped Jerry redecorate. He's rigged the place so he can watch me.

"You may wonder why you're being asked to walk through a maze," Jerry's voice echoes overhead. His tone is one dimensional and unaffected, as if he's reading from a script. "It's because you lack direction in life. I've been watching you, Cassandra. I've watched you-- watching others."

He knows I follow Mike, I think as I turn back the way I came, looking for a different direction that won't take me to a dead end.

"You need to find your own way instead of allowing

yourself to dangle in the wind, blown about by the whims of others. You need to carve your own path. And I believe, when you do-- you'll find it leads you to me. I am the one for you."

A shiver runs down my spine. *He thinks we're meant to be together.* At least Mike and I had a real relationship that spanned many months. I have good reason to believe we're meant for each other. Jerry's only known me a matter of weeks.

I pass by the first corridor, which I know leads back to the exit. I could leave the maze now and run from the store. But I think about the blood on the counter in the security store. What if Jerry's hurt someone and they need my help?

"I wouldn't do leave," Jerry's voice booms from over-head. He knows what I'm thinking. "It could cost you the man you want."

My heart beats in my chest. Jerry's kidnapped Mike. *The blood belonged to Mike.* He must be holding him hostage at the center of the maze. If I turn back now, I won't ever see him again. And I'll never know why Jerry's doing this to me.

A deep breath fuels my lungs with courage, and I head in the opposite direction, down a new corridor I haven't tried yet. At first, it looks like the others-- made from cardboard boxes-- but then, I notice something taped to the walls.

Photographs.

Pictures... of *me.*

Each photo has been printed in a glossy veneer, blown up into eight-by-tens. Some of them are black and white-- others, in full color. They've been taken at my most intimate moments. One picture is a candid of me slunk low in the driver's side of my car while following Mike, parked on the curb as I wait for him to exit a nearby business. Another was taken through the window of my apartment, the curtains ajar just enough to allow the camera lens a fleeting look at me, passing by the window-- shirtless-- a glass of wine in my hand. Another image shows me working at the Home Decor store, looking in the opposite direction as a customer asks me a question, my apron askew, hair piled on top of my head.

How did he get these?

"I want you to see yourself the way I see you," Jerry's voice echoes from overhead. "You are lost, Cassandra. What will it take to find you?"

My skin prickles as I continue through the labrynth, the number of photos increasing with every turn. Now, the pictures are ones from my past. Photos of me as a child. Pictures of me at summer camp. A family shot of me with my parents.

My parents. I stop at the photograph, running my hands over the smooth surface. What would they think about what I've done to Mike? Have I made him feel the same terror I'm feeling now?

The idea is too much to bear. I rip the photo off the wall and fold it in half, sticking it my pocket and soldiering on. As the pictures increase in frequency, I take it as a sign I'm headed in the right direction. If the photos decrease in frequency, I change direction.

And then-- I find it. The center of the maze. I know I've reached it because I round a corner, revealing a hundred-square-foot space free from boxes, reminding me of a clearing in the woods. The cement floor reaches out in all directions, and at the center of it, stands Jerry.

He's in front of a microphone that's been rigged to the ceiling, dangling down from a long cord. He's holding a paper, but that's not what's strange. What's strange is that his hands are tied together, and the look in his eyes is one I've never seen in him before: utter terror.

"I'm sorry," he says, and his whisper is carried across the room by the microphone. "I had to get back to my son. She said she has him--"

She? There's a long pause in which I wonder if Zoe found out what I was up to and decided to pursue me, but I shake the thought away. My hours of watching Zoe have taught me everything there is to know about her, and she's not a predator.

There's an eerie silence, and then the sound of footsteps echoes from a shadowed corridor of boxes behind the clearing in which Jerry stands. I recognize the combat boots at once. The nose piercing. The jet black hair.

"Patricia?" Her name comes out almost as a laugh. Her eyes flash and she looks offended. She clutches the gun she's holding tighter, her knuckles turning white at the edges.

"Didn't think I had it in me?" She snarls, tapping the gun against her temple to make her point.

"No, I just— didn't think you gave a shit about me," I shrug, still unable to believe that I'm standing here with my twenty-three-year-old maniacal boss.

Patricia laughs, a harsh, grating sound that bounces off the warehouse walls. "Didn't care? More like *you* didn't notice. Every time I invited you to a concert with me, you rejected me. I reached out, and you pushed me away. Because you don't want good things, Cassandra. There's a piece of you that wants to be unhappy."

Well, she's got me there, I think to myself.

"You never paid attention," Patricia continues. "Always so wrapped up in your own little world, chasing after Mike.

But you never saw the one person who was always there, always watching."

She steps forward, the gun aimed steadily at Jerry's head. "It's fitting that we have this conversation here, in the place where we shared so many intimate moments. And Jerry here, he was easy to manipulate. I showed up at the security store. Told him a sob story about trying to secure my house against an angry ex-boyfriend."

Jerry looks right at me, his eyes a pair of marbles in the dark— wide, and sad. "I'm sorry," he whispers. "She made me read the script. I wanted to warn you, but she said she has my son—"

"Quiet," Patricia snarls at him. "This isn't about *you*." She clears her throat like she's choking back sadness, and for a moment I wonder what her life is like. My mind scans our interactions for everything I know about Patricia. Her parents own the store, and they put her in charge. I get the impression she secretly hates them. She listens to heavy metal. She's always struck me as someone who feels alone in the world. That's all I know about Patricia.

I take a deep breath, trying to steady my nerves. "Patricia, you're right," I tell her, keeping my voice even. My hands raise in the air with the calm confidence of a hostage negotiator. "I never paid attention to you. Not really. And for that, I'm sorry. But it wasn't because you weren't enough. It was because of me. I'm a mess. I center my life around other people. I chase what I can't have. But that doesn't explain why you care. What do you *want*?"

"You," she says simply. "I want you to see me. To understand that we're meant to be together. You were supposed to fall in love with *me* through this process and instead— you got closer to him—" She pushes the gun against Jerry's temple.

My mind races. I need to disarm her, save Jerry, and get out of this warehouse alive. I glance around, searching for anything I can use as a weapon. There's nothing but the cardboard boxes and the contents within, which I can't see from here.

"Patricia," I say, feeling as if someone else is piloting my body. "You're right. I've been blind. But I see you now. Let Jerry go, and we can talk."

She hesitates, her eyes flickering with uncertainty. She's skeptical. She doesn't buy my story. Not yet.

"You and me? We're exactly alike," I tell her, hating that on some level, I know there's truth to my words. "We love people who don't even know we exist. We feel misunderstood by the world."

My legs shake as I take a step forward, reaching toward her with a gentle hand. My fingers trace the soft, plush skin of her cheek. "But you're not invisible anymore. I *see* you," I whisper. "You were right there. You were *always* right there."

She gazes at me. Her pupils widen in the dark. She wasn't lying when she said she liked me— the look of desire on her face says the girl has it bad. Out of the corner of my eye, I can just make out her arm holding the gun. It lowers slightly, pointing toward the floor rather than at Jerry.

"You're the *one*," I say, moving closer. My lips are almost on hers.

"I'm the one," she repeats.

"The one," I continue, leaning in as if I'm about to kiss her. "I can't wait to destroy."

In one smooth motion, I push Patricia to the floor. I'm on top of her, straddling her like a pro-wrestler. My fingers cut into her skin, grabbing her wrist on the side where she's holding the gun. I lift her arm into the air so hard it feels like I could wrench it from her body, then slam it back into the floor again, and again, and again. There's a sickening cracking sound that must be bone against cement. A howl escapes Patricia's lips. The gun goes off with a bang, and the bullet just misses me, whizzing across the warehouse.

I don't care. I'm an absolutely feral creature, and all the rage I've carried inside over the past two years is slipping out of me, an acid rain burning Patricia into the ground. I don't hate Patricia because she's been following me— I hate her because she's right. We *are* similar. And I want to eviscerate every piece of her that's like me in the hopes that I might, somehow, save myself. My teeth bite into her shoulder, chewing at her self-loathing. My left hand rips at her hair, pulling out a chunk of entitlement. My right hand continues slamming her arm against the cement floor until the gun slips from her fingers. She looks up at me, and for a second, her features become mine, and I'm looking in a mirror, fighting with myself. The room spins. A desperate desire to conquer myself bubbles like vomit in my throat. I bang my head against hers, shocked at how the hit reverberates through my skull. The shock puts us back in our rightful places, and now it's Patricia's surprised face looking up at me as she reaches one arm around to the back of her head. There's blood, there. She's banged it against the cement.

I grab the gun. My legs burn as I stand, limping toward Jerry. Together, we untie his hands. He's bleeding in the torso area, and for the first time, I notice that his face is covered in bruises. She's beat the shit out of him.

"You didn't see her coming?" I laugh at him. "Not a ringing endorsement for your security store."

He groans as he puts an arm around my shoulder. "Been thinking of getting into a different business actually," he says. "Maybe sell snorkels by the beach."

"If we make it out of here, I'm with you," I tell him. Together, we hobble back through the maze, trying to find our way through the twisted corridors. My heart pounds as I try to remember the way I came, but it's difficult to make sense of the labyrinth in front of me.

Finally, we reach the exit of the maze, spilling out into the main warehouse. A crackling sound echoes from overhead. It's Patricia's voice in the loudspeaker. "I'll never stop," she says, her voice breaking. "You can't leave me because we are the same."

Her words stop me in my tracks. *We are the same.* Jerry's speaking to me, but I can't make out what he's saying. He's gesturing frantically at the exit, but I ignore him, my eyes landing on the forklift by the door.

I walk toward it and hop on, turning the key over in the ignition.

We are the same.

Patricia's words echo in my ears as I throw the lift into gear. It roars to life, charging toward the full cardboard boxes that constitute the maze. I aim for the center and charge toward the labyrinth. The forklift hits the boxes with a crunching sound. To my left and right, heavy items fall to the ground, one after the other. Lamps. Couches. Credenzas. Tables. Wood shatters, but I keep moving the forklift forward, barely shielded by the cover overhead.

I only stop when I hear Patricia's scream fade. Then, I give the accelerator some gas and push the forklift forward a little further for good measure. It's a move that costs me. A couch from overhead comes hurtling straight down onto the lift, and I'm submerged in a blissful, black, crunching darkness.

"THE ONE"

S he's buried me. The boxes pin me down. I never thought it would end this way. Why can't she see that I love her? Why can't she love me back?

Is there anyone who loves me back?

CASSANDRA

Patricia's parents are the first ones at the scene, miraculously arriving even sooner than the first responders. They're a worried pair, the two of them tussled and groggy, still in their pajamas. I overhear Patricia's mother tell an EMT that they live an hour away. They saw her on the store security camera behaving oddly, and they knew something was wrong. Apparently, they've known for a long time that something was wrong. "She stays in her room all day when she's not at the store," Patricia's mother tells the Police Officer that's taking her statement. "She sits in front of the computer. We try— I promise, we try." There's a pleading edge to her voice, like she wishes the Police Officer would tell her this isn't their fault— that they aren't bad parents. If he thinks as much, he doesn't say it out loud.

They've brought two ambulances to the scene, their flashing lights painting the night red. In the back of the first ambulance, Patricia lays on a stretcher, her injured right arm handcuffed to its metal bars. She doesn't say a word, no matter how many questions the officers ask her. She isn't cooperating. It's as if she's a computer that's been shut down, the screen in her eyes frozen in place.

In the second ambulance, I'm seated next to Jerry, watching as an EMT wraps the wound on his torso. They've told us it's the result of blunt force trauma. But he'll be okay.

"I should've found a way to get out of this without involving you," Jerry says, looking up at me from the stretcher. "I read the script she gave me, but I should have fought—" I wave a hand in the air like it doesn't matter, even though we both know that it does. Jerry allowed Patricia to use him as bait. To lure me into the maze. Whatever beautiful little thing that was blossoming between us has begun to wilt. It's nobody's fault. Not really. Just one of those unexplainable times when something that could have been good goes to pieces. Love is like that. A bowl on a potter's wheel that looks so promising, until one wrong move is made, and the whole thing turns to mush.

"You thought she had your son," I say graciously. "Anyone would have done the same thing."

Jerry doesn't answer, but looks down at the ambulance floor, shame fleeting across his features. Upon hearing our story, the Police immediately did a wellness check on Jerry's son and found that he was safe in his bed at home, with Jerry's ex. Patricia lied. Simple as that.

"Still," Jerry said, and I nod before he can add anything else.

Still.

"When Patricia said you two are the same," Jerry adds. "What did she mean?" He's looking at me like he suspects me. Like he's never seen me before. Apparently the spell between us has worn off in both directions.

"She meant that I'm no good," I tell him. "And she's right."

His eyebrows arch in surprise. The moment should upset me, but instead, there's something healing about it. It's as if I'm sucking poison from a wound— Jerry is getting to know the real me, just like he should have, from day one. I felt him watch me when I attacked Patricia. I saw the way his expression changed when I was beating her into the cement warehouse floor like a bug beneath my shoe. It doesn't matter that I did it to save both our lives. It's a moment Jerry can't unsee.

I lean in, wrapping my arms around Jerry's neck. "It's been fun," I tell him. Then, I kiss him, slow at first, then feral, just like the me I left back in the warehouse. I bite his lip before we separate so he knows how lucky he is that I'm about to leave him alone forever. "Take care of what matters," I tell him, nodding at the cell phone by his side. He's left it out on the stretcher, and the lockscreen is a picture of his son.

"You got somewhere important to be?" Jerry smiles at me, but the smile doesn't make it to his eyes. It's a half-hearted attempt to save what we were starting to build. I admire that he doesn't give up so easy. "It's just," he pauses. "I feel like I'm never going to see you again."

If only you knew how badly I don't want that to be true, I think. But it's time. Jerry has his son to think about. If tonight proved anything, it's that my presence only brings trouble. But I've never been good at letting go of a connection. My hobby of following Mike proves that well enough. It couldn't hurt to leave a door open.

"I'll try to check in on you every now and then," I tell him. He offers a weak nod. He doesn't know what a bullet he has dodged. I stand, finding my own way out of the ambulance's open back doors, taking one last look at Jerry over my shoulder. This is the last time he'll see me. But it might not be the last time I see him. If I want to watch him, I will.

My sneakers hit the asphalt and the messy scene expands before me, yellow crime tape everywhere and Police Officers weaving around each other like ants. I'm tempted to leave the whole thing behind and disappear, but something in me wants to talk to her. To Patricia. The person who saw me when I wasn't watching.

I walk toward the second ambulance, letting myself in the back doors. A well-meaning EMT starts to protest. "You can't—" he says, but I cut him off.

"She wants to talk to me," I nod at Patricia, who's still laying frozen on her gurney. "Don't you?" I ask.

There's a silent moment while she thinks about it, and then she nods in agreement. "She's the only one I want to talk to," Patricia says.

I sit on a metal storage compartment, looking over the EMT's shoulder.

"Your parents say you spend a lot of time alone in your room," I say. Patricia nods. She doesn't look twenty-three. In this moment, she doesn't even look like the boss who made my life hell at work. Instead, she looks like a scared teenager.

"So what?" she shrugs, seeming even more like a child. She's an easy case to crack. She just needs someone to talk some sense into her.

"So," I tell her, leaning in so she can hear me better. "You think you and me are alike? You're not wrong. You're on the path to become me. But you still have time to save yourself."

She blinks, surprised at how direct I am.

"What if I don't want to save myself?" She says, her eyes

watering as she glances up at the ceiling, still defiant and unyielding.

"Then let me help you," I smile. "If I ever catch you following me, or anyone else again, I will rip you limb from limb. I will climb into your bedroom window when you least expect it and drug you with a sedative, then take you to my own private warehouse and show you exactly what I do with people who fuck with me—"

"Woah," the EMT says, stopping his fiddling with the IV in his hand.

"You mind your fucking business," I snarl at him. "We're talking here. Aren't we Patricia? This is what you wanted, isn't it? To play with the big girls? Are you fucking scared of me? Because the women you meet in prison won't be any better. Time to start learning right now, don't you think?"

She's crying now, and giant tears spill over her eyes in tragic puddles.

"Give me a fucking break," I laugh at her. "Tears? *Really?* You're scared now? Well let me scare you even more. Your destiny rests with two people. Me... and him," I point out the ambulance windows at the second rig, its back doors still open, revealing Jerry. "Now, I happen to know that Jerry has a son. And he'll take it easy on you, because he'll see you as a kid. He won't campaign for prison. But me? I could let you rot. I'll write a letter asking the judge to give you twenty years. And why shouldn't I?"

"I don't know," Patricia says, her tears catching in her voice. "Just do it then."

I shake my head. "No, I won't," I tell her. "Because I'm going to watch over you myself. And I think we both know, I'm an excellent watcher. You step one toe out of line to ruin your own life, and I'll handle it instead of leaving it up to saner, better people among us, like this guy," I nod at the

EMT, who's back to playing with the IV. He looks concerned, but doesn't say anything.

"I thought you would understand me," Patricia says. "I thought you would see who I am and love me back. Nobody loves me back." She's sobbing now, and I put my hands on her cheeks, squeezing a little too hard as I force her to look out the ambulance window.

"See them? Right there?" I'm pointing her gaze toward her parents, who are talking frantically with the Police Chief, no doubt spinning a story that their daughter is mentally ill and couldn't help herself. They're laying the groundwork to get her the lightest sentence possible, because they've spoiled her for her entire life. And they're not going to stop now. "They love you back. Why don't you start there?"

Her eyes widen as the truth of it all hits her.

"And if you don't turn it around for their sake, or even yours, remember... I'll be watching." I smack her, *hard*, on the cheek, and the spot turns red.

"Hey!" The EMT shouts, but I'm already backing away.

I hope I've scared her straight, but it's too soon to tell. I'll have to check in on her when she doesn't expect it— maybe a few weeks from now. I make a mental note to see how far away her house is from Mike's apartment.

"I don't want to be anything like you!" Patricia shouts at me, pulling on the cuffs that keep her arms stuck to the gurney.

Perfect, I smile, glad to have achieved what I hoped. My body feels lighter as I stand, waltzing out of the ambulance, letting the doors shut hard behind me.

I'm back on the parking lot asphalt again, looking out across the tiny strip mall. Nobody notices as I step away from the scene. Not the police. Not Jerry. Not even Patricia's parents, who are still talking to the officer, gesturing wildly, their arms making stories in the air.

I take one last look at them all, thinking about how much better it is to do the watching than it is to be watched.

Patricia's words play on repeat in mind:

Nobody loves me back.

The words should make me sad, but all I feel is a strange sort of numbness. It's like I've met myself all over again, and been given the chance to start anew. I want to believe that this time I'll do better, but I know how these things go— I've made myself too many broken promises to take the new ones seriously.

I'll just have to see which way the wind blows me.

CASSANDRA

ONE MONTH LATER

It's funny how time can change the way you see something.

It's been one month since the night at the warehouse, and everything I thought I was afraid of has come to pass.

Mike and Zoe are together. Not in the fragile, budding way that can so easily be destroyed, but in the solid, firm way that turns two people into one. I'm not sure they're aware of it yet, but they're a unit. They've become a single entity, born from the fragments of who they each used to be.

I thought I would be sad to see Mike move on, but I'm not. I'm at peace with it. I've settled into my role as the third person in their relationship, watching them from afar. Some nights, I sit in my car outside Mike's place, eating a cheeseburger in the driver's seat, watching the two of them have a meal together in Mike's kitchen. I've learned so much about Zoe since we all first met. I thought I would hate her, but I've grown to feel a kind of warmth for her— the same warmth I feel for Mike. She's given me a renewed sense of purpose. When Mike is away or delivering furniture too far outside of town, Zoe gives me someone else to watch. I've heard people say that when a friend finds a partner, you get two for the price of one. I feel that way about Zoe, now that we've gotten to know each other better.

I like to believe I had a hand in bringing them together. Trauma bonds people and the discovery that they were being watched seemed to bring Zoe and Mike closer. Really, Mike should be sending me a thank you card. He might never have landed a catch like Zoe without my help.

They called the Police of course— after they found the cameras in Zoe's place. I wasn't surprised when an officer showed up at my door, a badge pinned to his uniform. But when he found out I'd had a stalker of my own, the story was muddled, and I became the victim. "You were the woman at the warehouse?" He asked me, mouth dropped open in shock. Apparently the entire department had told the story of what happened at the Home Decor store. "That was one of the weirdest calls we'd had in a while," he said, his tone of voice implying I should be proud of my involvement.

I nodded, leaning against the doorframe of my apartment, allowing my pajama robe to slip open a little, my waif-like body a tool to be used in this moment. "It was really awful," I said. "I can see why Mike thought it was me spying on him given how bad our breakup was, but clearly it was the girl was following *me*. It's so tragic that we're all tangled up in her mess."

Mike pushed to have the Police question me further— I know, because I heard him make the call while sitting outside his apartment. But they refused. They said they couldn't do anything without more evidence.

Zoe reconnected with her father, the mysterious *W*. I made sure I was present for the little brunch they arranged in Silverlake. It was at a cute, bistro-style restaurant. Zoe didn't see me, hidden behind a newspaper, enjoying a coffee on the patio. But I saw her. I watch her cry, and also laugh. She gave him a hug at the end. I don't know what will come from it all, but I know that I'll be there for her.

Patricia, up until this point, seems to have avoided jail. There's been one hearing at an intimidating, multi-story court house in downtown. I didn't attend. Instead, I sent a written letter. I asked the judge to take it easy on her. Patricia was right about one thing: if there's one person who understands how she feels, it's me. The lawyer handling the case has called me a couple times. He said her parents are angling to get her into treatment instead of prison. Good for her.

I heard from the lawyer that Jerry agrees with a sentence that involves counseling. I haven't watched Jerry, because I like to him too much to feed the addiction. He's better off without me. And besides, I already have Mike.

Mike.

Now, I'm sitting on the rooftop of the building across the street from Mike's apartment, thinking about everything that's happened in the past few weeks. I love this angle, because I can see into his bedroom and bathroom. He's closed the curtains, but there's a little sliver in the gap where the sides meet. Every now and then he walks past it, and I get a glimpse of his face.

It's a hard face to let go of.

It's one I'll probably *never* be able to let go of. But there's a piece of me that wonders if things would have lasted between us if I could have healed myself. Patricia taught me that love is different than ownership. It's a hard concept to grasp. The people who love you are the ones who never give up on you, but Mike gave up on me. I don't know what I'm supposed to do with that.

My fingers rummage through the pocket of my sweatshirt and I pull out the picture I ripped off the walls of the maze Patricia constructed. It's me, as a child, at a theme park with my parents. A crease where I've folded it in half runs through the middle.

I think about the bravery it took for Zoe to meet with her Dad, and then take a deep breath, doing what I know I have to do. I pull out my cell phone, dialing the number for my childhood home. It's one I haven't called in ages. They don't call me either, but not because they aren't trying. I've changed my number so many times, I'm unfindable.

There's a ringing noise, and then the line clicks on.

"I'm ready to come home," I say, before the person on the other line can speak. I'm not sure if it's my Mom or Dad who picked up, but it doesn't matter— one will tell the other. "I want to fix things, for real this time."

In the moment, I mean it. I know I *will* fly home. And they'll try to get me help. It might work, for awhile.

But then I stare back at Mike's window, and the curtains flutter. It's the tiniest movement, but it sparks something in me. His face passes by again and he stops in his tracks, then looks out the window, straight towards me, as if he can sense that I'm here. Untouchable. Slight, and ephemeral.

No matter where I go— no matter where I run to— there will always be something between us. Mike, and me— a woman in the wind.

~

THANK *you for reading the Predator / Prey thriller series!*

FOR MORE FROM *author Valerie Brandy, look for "Murder Behind the Gates," Book One in the Private Investigator Annie Hudson Mystery Series. Available now in paperback, ebook, and audiobook.*

MORE FROM VALERIE BRANDY

AVAILABLE NOW:

The Private Investigator

Annie Hudson Real Estate Mystery Series

- "Murder Behind the Gates" — The Private Investigator Annie Hudson Real Estate Mystery Series, Book One
- "Murder in the Penthouse" — The Private Investigator Annie Hudson Real Estate Mystery Series, Book Two
- "Murder on the Farm" — The Private Investigator Annie Hudson Real Estate Mystery Series, Book Three

The Predator / Prey Thriller Series

- "Trail of Obsession" — The Predator / Prey Thriller Series, Book One
- "Lies Run Deep" — The Predator / Prey Thriller Series, Book Two
- "The Trap is Set" — The Predator / Prey Thriller Series, Book Four

LETTER FROM THE AUTHOR

Dear Reader,

Thank you for dedicating your time to the Predator/Prey thriller series! I'm a screenwriter and filmmaker coming to books from Film & TV, but one thing I love about books in particular, is connecting directly with a community of readers. It's very special to be able to speak with you and hear what you want from characters in our novels.

I hope you'll reach out to me by joining my mailing list at the link below! I'm always releasing new books, and love to keep my readers updated on new releases, advanced copies, free giveaways of novellas, sneak previews, and more.

If you liked this series, I hope you'll check out my Annie Hudson Private Investigator Real Estate Mystery Series, which starts with book one, "Murder Behind the Gates."

And if you want to read more from me in general, please keep in touch by signing up for my mailing list at the link below! I love hearing from readers, which makes all the work of writing worthwhile.

Warmly,

— Valerie Brandy

www.valeriebrandy.com

Scan this code to visit the author's website!

ACKNOWLEDGMENTS

To everyone I thanked in book one. You have my continued appreciation, love, and dedication.

Valerie Brandy is a writer, direc-
tor, and actress based in Los
Angeles.

She began her writing career by
selling a feature length screen-
play at just 20 years old,
becoming one of the youngest
members of the WGA west at
the time. She's since written for
numerous film studios and television networks, most recently
serving as a full time staff writer at Walt Disney Studios live
action feature department, where she continues to develop
new projects. Her work has been acknowledge by the
Nichol Fellowships in Screenwriting, run by the Academy
of Arts & Sciences.

Her directorial feature film debut, *Lola's Last Letter*— which
she also wrote and starred in— was released in 2016 by
Random Media and Sony's "The Orchard" after a successful
festival run, premiering at the historic Chinese Theatre in
Hollywood. The film received a five-star review from the
Examiner, a special feature in Huffington Post, and a Best
Principal Actress nomination from Los Angeles Film
Review. Valerie shot the film in seven days with a cast and

crew of just seven people. In their review of the film, Huffington post stated that, "... the key word in describing Brandy is *unflinching*..." Starpulse called the film, "... breathtakingly real and raw... Brandy is an important voice for her generation." *Lola's Last Letter* is currently available OnDemand at iTunes, Vudu, Googleplay, Comcast, Youtube, and many other platforms.

Brandy's second feature film, "A Unified Theory of Love," stars Richard Karn (*Home Improvement*) and Eric Isenwhoer (*Parks & Rec)*, and is due to hit the festival circuit in 2024.

As an actress, Valerie recurred on FX's Emmy-winning show "Justified" as the manipulative Trixie. She received her B.A. from UCLA in three years, graduating as a prestigious Alumni Scholarship Recipient, and holds an M.F.A. in Film & Television Production from Asbury University, where she graduated Magna Cum Laude.

Brandy lives in the greater Los Angeles area with her smush-faced dog and snow-white cat.

www.ingramcontent.com/pod-product-compliance
Lightning Source LLC
Chambersburg PA
CBHW030143010826
48973CB00002B/706